# THE SPANKING ACADEMY

First published in the United Kingdom in 2011
by Miro Books



ISBN 978-1-906320-31-7

Typeset by Miro Books
Printed and bound in the UK & US
A catalogue record of this book is available
from the British Library

Cover design by Miro Books

# THE SPANKING ACADEMY

JACQUI KNIGHT

# CHAPTER ONE

I shivered as David put his hand under my skirt and groped inside my panties. This was the second time that we'd got together for sex, but the first time we'd actually taken the risk of doing it inside my boarding academy. We were allowed to entertain parents and friends on the weekends and I'd managed to smuggle him up to my bedroom.

Keira, the girl I shared the room with had agreed in advance to make herself scarce and my parents were occupied talking to the headmistress, Miss Reynolds. So the coast was clear and I was able to enjoy spending some time in bed with my good looking boyfriend. And I needed a fuck, oh yes, it had been four weeks since we'd been together and I was as horny as hell. A dildo was ok, but sooner or later a girl needed the real thing, well, this one sure did. His fingers found my cunt and a couple of them pushed inside, I stiffened with pleasure feeling the dampness come flooding into my vagina as my arousal began to really go wild. I shouldn't have been doing this, I knew. Mom and Dad were here to have a long talk with Miss Reynolds, my behaviour had been, shall we say, not quite up to the standards expected of refined young ladies attending this Academy. That was the official version, the truth was I'd been an absolute bitch, twice brought back drunk to the Academy by police after evenings out at nightclubs in the local town. I'd been insubordinate to the staff, so they said. If telling them to 'fuck off' when I got tired of their constant whining was insubordination then I guess it would be true. Yet I did work hard, it's just that I was a seventeen year old girl, a teenager who wanted to experience a little of what life had to offer, maybe a lot of what life had to offer, without being told off every time I did something they didn't like.

David was pulling my panties and pantyhose down now, they came off my legs and wearing only my short Academy skirt I lay down on my back and waited for him to remove his pants and shorts. His cock sprang out, it looked delicious, hot, throbbing and all mine.

"Fuck me, David, I need you so bad, get it inside me," I said desperately.

He laughed. "You're bloody hot for me today, Abbey, is this place getting to you?"

"You're damn right it is, I can't seem to do anything right, all I get is constant...Ohh."

His shaft rammed into me, Christ it was hard and big, it felt wonderful. I lifted up my legs and wrapped them around his body, holding him to me, forever, if possible. He started to fuck me and I closed my eyes, losing myself to the blissful pleasure of the moment. All of the pressure drained away from me, the tension and the unhappiness that made my life at Academy so miserable. I was no longer in my room at the Academy, I was transported, I fantasized that we were in a hut perched on some South Pacific beach. I was a dusky maiden, ok, a horny maiden and David was a hard, young native boy, initiating me into womanhood. He was certainly hard and young, his lovemaking set me on fire and I began to pant with joy and sexual arousal, lost for all time to the passion of the sex in this place where there was so little passion. It happened too quickly but I couldn't stop myself, I started to come to a climax, my mind thrilling to the wonder of the moment, then I was there, screaming, shrieking with pleasure and David was still fucking me, he hadn't come yet, Christ, I was going to have a second climax, this was fantastic, joyous.

"What the hell is going on?"

Despite the danger of someone coming into my room and catching us, I felt a moment of terrible loss and sadness as David pulled his cock out of me and leapt off the bed. He was hopping around, trying to pull his shorts and pants back on. I covered my naked fanny with my hands and looked up. Dear God, no. Miss Reynolds, the headmistress, Mom and Dad were standing behind her looking at me with a shocked expression on their faces. There was a frozen moment when no-one knew what to do or say. Then the headmistress muttered, "You'd better come and see me in my office," then she whirled away. I heard my mom speaking to my dad.

"Charles, would you give us a few moments, I'll deal with this and then we'd better go and square it with the headmistress."

"Jesus Christ, what a mess," he said, then disappeared.

David had just about got himself decent. "I really am sorry, Mrs Gilmore," he said to my mom. His face was comical, bright red with shame and embarrassment.

"Get out, David," she said to him. "I don't want to hear your apology, just get out and don't come back."

"Yeah, sure, sorry, I'll go away then."

He rushed out of the room without even saying goodbye to me. I guess I couldn't blame him, my mom was blazing with anger. It was my turn now to feel the heat.

"What do you think you're doing, Abbey? Are you totally out of your mind?"

Several answers went through my mind, but none of them were suitable to the occasion.

"I'm sorry, Mom, it won't happen again."

"What? Do you think I believe that, you've gone totally

crazy lately, Abbey. Getting home drunk late at night, swearing at the teachers, now this, sex in an Academy, of all places. And if that isn't bad enough, haven't you heard of HIV and AIDS? Venereal disease, unwanted pregnancies, I noticed that David wasn't using a condom."

"Mom!" I said, shocked that she'd seen his erect penis.

"Don't Mom me, young lady. I could hardly fail to notice that he wasn't wearing a condom, you weren't very discreet, either of you. You'd better get dressed now, we'll need to go and see the headmistress, I thought we'd straightened everything out, we were coming to tell you that provided your behaviour improved you could stay at the Academy. I guess we'll need to relook at that agreement."

"Whatever," I said carelessly. I didn't want to stay at this stupid Academy, it was boring, every day seemed like a month. I pulled on my panties and pantyhose and smoothed my skirt down. Then I went to the bathroom, washed my fanny and redid my face in the mirror. They didn't like girls wearing makeup, but I was seventeen, not seven, so fuck'em. I fastened my hair down with a hair band and went to join my mom. She was still standing where I'd left her.

"I'm ready, shall we get this over with?"

"You'd better put your blazer on, Abbey, at least try and make an effort."

"If you like." I pulled on my blazer and we walked out of the door and along the corridor. We went down the main stairs and out to the front entrance, just inside the hallway was the headmistress's office, dad was already outside, waiting for us.

"All set?" he asked.

Mom nodded. He knocked on the door, I heard a terse 'enter', and we went in. She was sitting behind a carved wooden desk with a file open in front of her. My file, obviously. My parents were invited to sit, I had to stand next to them, my feet together, hands folded demurely by my side, the picture of the timid, repentant girl. I hoped it would be enough, although I didn't want to stay at the Academy, but neither did I want to suffer the shit that would fly if I was expelled. The first words that the headmistress uttered put paid to that notion.

"I'm afraid I have to expel you, Abbey. Your parents persuaded me that your behaviour would improve, but clearly that is not the case. I would like you out of the Academy by the end of the day."

My parents were silent for a few moments, I suppose they had used up every argument earlier to keep me here, they couldn't think of any more. My dad couldn't help but vent his frustration.

"Damnit, Abbey, why are you behaving so badly, what's gone wrong?"

I shrugged. I was a teenager, so what else was new?

"Couldn't you have disciplined her more?" he asked the headmistress. "It seems to me that kids these days get let off everything so lightly. Couldn't you have been a lot tougher with her? In my day, she'd have been given several whacks with the cane, that would have sorted her out."

Miss Reynolds smiled and shook her head. "We can't do that, Mr Gilmore, even though some of us think it would make for better behaved children and a higher standard of discipline in the Academy. Frankly, it's just not condoned any more in places like this. Well, not in most educational establishments anyway."

He seized on that. "What do you mean, most educational establishments? Does that mean that there are some places that are stricter with their discipline, that maybe use corporal punishment in the worst cases like our daughter?"

She didn't answer for a moment, I could see her thinking. "There is one that I know of," she answered. "It's called 'The Academy', but I really don't know much about it. It's in Scotland somewhere, I think it's on an island. Parents do send their young women there as a last resort. We've had a couple of girls that have been sent there, all I know is when they come back they are completely changed. They have a better attitude to and work they behave themselves, the transformation is remarkable. But their methods are, I believe, very unconventional."

"You mean they use corporal punishment?" Mom asked.

She nodded. "I believe so, yes, amongst other things.

It's a kind of boot camp, an academy of last resort for girls, well, frankly, girls like Abbey whose lives are spiralling downwards out of control."

They were talking about this as if I wasn't in the room.

"Hey, don't I get to say a word or two about this? I'm not going to some crappy Academy in the wilds of Scotland, I want to stay here."

"You can't stay here," Mom said sharply. "I think you've had enough chances. You'd better go and pack your things, bring your suitcase down when you're ready to leave. We'll talk it over with Miss Reynolds and see what other options are open to us."

"Ok, Mom, I'll go and pack my things." I decided to leave them to it, as long as they didn't try and send me off to some dump in Scotland. It would be simple enough to get out of, they could try but I would just refuse to go. I'd sooner go to the local college on some crummy estate than a boot camp outfit for wayward girls. I could imagine it, early nights, early mornings and cold showers. No thanks. I went up to my room and packed my case. I did feel a bit of a pang at leaving, I hadn't liked the place but some of the kids were ok, besides, I hated the idea of being thrown out. Again. I lugged the case back downstairs and knocked on the headmistress's door.

Mom opened it. "We're all finished, dear. We're leaving now, I don't think the headmistress is keen to say goodbye, she's a bit upset at your behaviour, especially when she's tried so hard with you."

I shrugged. "She can suit herself, the miserable fucking old bat."

Mom frowned. "Abbey, why do you do that, use that awful language? It's terrible for a well brought up young lady to speak like that."

"Whatever," I replied. Dad came out of the office, thanked the headmistress and took my case. We got into the car and drove to our family home in Maidenhead, a prosperous and dull town a few miles outside of London. They were quiet as we travelled, I couldn't help but wonder what they were thinking, what did they have in mind for me?

"Well, what are you planning to do, are you going to tell me?" I asked them eventually. Was that a guilty look I saw go between them?

"We haven't decided yet, darling," Mom said. "The Academy, the place that the headmistress mentioned, sounds like a very good idea, she said it could do you the world of good."

No way, Jose, I thought to myself. "Sorry, Mom, but if that's what you and Dad have got in mind you can forget it."

"We'll see, my darling," she said, but she sounded worried. Was something going on here that I didn't know about? Well, it really didn't make any difference, they could enrol me in any college they liked, but if I didn't like the idea of it the answer would simply be no.

We got home to our neat detached house and I went to put my things away in my room. I changed out of my school uniform into my denim jeans and a black Iron Maiden T-shirt, then booted up my computer. I was browsing through my Facebook pages when Mom called from downstairs.

"Abbey, would you come down here, there's someone we'd like you to meet."

"Ok, give me a moment."

I switched everything off, I didn't want them snooping around the kind of things I talked about online. Then I went downstairs.

"Abbey, we'd like you to meet Mr Murdoch, Mr Julian Murdoch, he's come here to talk about your training."

"What? On a Saturday evening, what's going on here?" I asked her. I was puzzled, who the hell was this guy? He was staring at me with a confident, amused smile on his face. Well, he could wipe that off for starters. I spoke to him directly.

"What do you do then Mr Murdoch? Some kind of educational advisor? You must be pretty desperate for work to turn out on a Saturday evening."

He smiled even more broadly at my barb, pity, he should have been annoyed, I'd have to try harder.

"Or maybe you're an errand boy, which is it?" I continued. But he smiled wider still.

"Miss Gilmore, I am the headmaster of The Academy, I understand you've heard of us."

That shook me. The place in Scotland, the boot camp for naughty young women.

"I've heard of you and your Academy, Mr Murdoch. But I'm afraid you've come a long way for nothing."

His eyebrows rose. "Really? I think your parents are very keen for you to join our little establishment for a short time at least."

I looked at them. "Is that true, Mom and Dad? You're not seriously suggesting I go to this Godforsaken place?"

"We think it's for the best, Abbey, something needs to be done about you."

I lost my cool then. "Is that so? Well fuck you, both of you, and fuck you too, Mr Murdoch, I suggest you go back to Scotland and suck your dick. I'm going back to my bedroom, I've got more important things to get on with."

I went to leave the room but a woman was stood in my way, she was dressed like some kind of a nurse. She blocked the doorway and took hold of my arm, a firm, strong grip.

"Let me go, you fucking whore," I shouted.

Murdoch came alongside me and took my other arm.

"We're sorry, Abbey," I heard Mom say. "It's for the best, you've got to do something about your behaviour, you're just not the girl we used to know. Go with them to The Academy and do exactly as they say. We'll see you in three months time."

Three fucking months? "Let me go, you bastards, I'm going back to my bedroom," I screamed, but they dragged me out of the house and into a car. I was pitched into the back seat and the nurse, some kind of a throwback to the Nazi era, got in with me and held me firmly as the doors shut.

I flung myself against the opposite door to try to open it but the child locks were on and it wouldn't budge. I went to open the window, but the handle was missing, the bastards seemed to have thought of everything. I could see my parents standing at the front door of the house, looking white faced and anxious. "Let me fucking go, you shits, let me go, I'll report you for kidnap."

They totally ignored me, it was as if I hadn't spoken. The car drove out of Maidenhead and onto the motorway heading north. I put my head in my hands and wept, I felt totally powerless, but resolved to get away from these fuckers as soon as an opportunity presented itself. I was shaking with rage, weeping tears of frustration and misery, perhaps with a good measure of fear as well. Then I felt a prick as something touched my arm. I looked up quickly, the nurse had injected me with something.

"What the fuck was that, you nasty cow?" I asked her sharply.

But she just smiled. "You just lay back and rest, dear. You'll need your energy for later, just relax."

"I don't want to fucking relax you evil old bat, I want to..."

But my head started to swim and I felt muzzy. The car seemed to become vague and indistinct, I felt so tired. As I went to sleep I heard her say, "It's ok, she's gone."

## CHAPTER TWO

I awoke to the feeling of movement, I was laying on some kind of narrow bed, everything was moving up and down. A boat, of course, I was on a boat. I looked down at myself, I was still dressed as I had been at the house, jeans and a t-shirt. I shivered, it was cold, so cold. Where the hell was I? I got up, my legs felt rubbery but I managed to steady myself against the motion of the boat and went up three steps to a door that led into the cockpit of the vessel. I opened the door and went through, there was a wind blowing, light rain falling and I put my arms around me to stop the shivering. Julian Murdoch was sitting on a seat at the rear of the small craft, it must have been about thirty feet long. The nurse was sitting next to him, a tough looking guy of about thirty was steering the boat.

"Look, what the fuck's going on here?" I asked Murdoch.

"We're taking you to The Academy, Miss Gilmore."

"But, why the boat ride?"

He looked surprised. "Because it's on an island, of course, why else?"

I shook my head, trying to clear it. So it was true, my parents had sent me to a boarding academy on some remote island, Christ, it couldn't get any worse.

"Look, I'm freezing, have you got something I can wear, I'm getting soaked too, it's raining?"

He called over to the nurse. "Miss Bowles, would you pass Abbey a waterproof coat, please."

She nodded and went into the cabin and came back with a bright yellow rubber raincoat, complete with hood.

"This is what the girls where, put it on and make sure you fasten the hood," she said sternly.

I looked at her. "I don't want to fasten the fucking hood, I just want the coat to keep myself dry."

She smiled, but there was no humour there. "Academy rules, Abbey. If you wear the coat, you wear it with the hood up, do you want the coat or not?"

I took the raincoat without a word and put it on and zipped it up to the neck, pulled the hood over my head and fastened the hood with drawstrings that tied under my chin. The coat was cold and smelt of rubber, but at least it kept the worst of the weather off me. I stood looking out at the sea, in the distance I could see a low island about half a mile away. Looking back I could see the mainland, about a mile behind us. So the Academy was about a mile and a half offshore, shit, that would make it difficult to get away. I'd obviously have to make myself as obnoxious as possible to get them to expel me again. I laughed inside, little did they know who they were getting at their precious Academy.

The boat docked at a small jetty and I climbed off behind Murdoch and the nurse, whose name I gathered was Nurse Charlotte Bowles, I'd overheard the headmaster taking to her. We walked up a path to The Academy, a building about four hundred yards away. It was a grim, grey Victorian structure. The only people I could see were wearing yellow slickers like the one I had on, several groups of two or three of them walking around the moorland that surrounded The Academy. Great, what a dump. Cold, wet, miserable and isolated. The sooner I got away from here the better. We walked through the main entrance and the two led me down a dark dingy corridor and through a door into a room like a waiting room.

"Sit down," Murdoch said quietly, pointing to a chair.

I let out a great sigh to show him that I wasn't impressed, then slumped in a chair, still wearing my slicker, it was almost as cold inside the building as it had been outside. Nurse Bowles stood watching me as the head went away and came back a few minutes later with a pale looking girl of about my age, the first pupil I had seen. She was wearing some kind of Academy uniform, a short skirt and blouse and was carrying a bundle of clothes.

"This is Olivia Stern, Abbey. She is to be your mentor, she'll explain everything to you and what to do. First of all, you need to get changed, after that you can go to your dormitory."

I gave him a nasty look. "My friend, if you think I'm getting changed into some crappy uniform you've got another think coming. I want out of here and as quickly as possible."

He shrugged. "Come on, Nurse Bowles. We'll leave them to it. Olivia, explain the rules to Abbey, after that it's up to her. We'll be back to let you out in half an hour, you can show her up to the dormitory then."

They went out of the room and I heard the key turning in the door. I looked at Olivia.

"Ok, what's the deal here, what am I missing?"

"Abbey, you're making a big mistake. Don't underestimate these people. Get into uniform and learn to keep your mouth shut and do as you're told."

I looked at her incredulously. "What's the matter with you, surely you don't just do as these people say? Don't you ever fight back?"

She laughed bitterly. "You don't fight back here if you know what's good for you. They use the cane, a lot. Have you ever been severely caned on the bottom, right in front of the whole assembly, tied to a vaulting horse on The Academy stage?"

I burst out laughing. "Look, I know when you're trying to have a laugh, now tell me the real deal here."

"That is the real deal, I'm not joking," she replied.

I grinned. "In that case I'll tell them to go fuck themselves, I'm not wearing their stupid uniform."

"Look, don't you see?" she continued. "They'll take your own clothes from you soon anyway, if you refuse to wear uniform they'll be quite happy to see you go around naked, they don't give a shit. You'll freeze your arse off in this place, even with the clothes on they give us it's always cold."

"What are these people, some kind of sadists or perverts?" I asked wonderingly.

She nodded. "Now you're getting it. That's exactly what they are. We're all here because we refused to knuckle down at our previous places. Our parents send us here to be disciplined, nothing else. That's what they do. Abbey, you really should get into uniform, honestly, you'll be punished if you don't, and I'm talking about a caning, as well as freezing your tits off in this hellhole with nothing on, believe me, they will do it."

I thought for a few moments. Then I shrugged and unzipped the rubber slicker, loosened the hood and pulled it off. Reluctantly I took off my T-shirt, shoes and jeans and put my hands out to take the clothing.

"No, Abbey, all of it, the underwear as well. They won't allow you to keep anything you bring here, everything has to be supplied by the Academy."

I felt my anger boiling over, but it wasn't the time to resist, or the person to get angry with, Olivia was just telling it to me as it was for everyone. Not to worry, sister, I'd arrived. I'll sort them out later. I took off my bra and panties, the other girl handed me the bundle of clothing. The first shock was the bra, an ill-fitting garment made of heavy cotton. I fastened it over my breasts and rummaged around for the panties. All I could find was a pair of large, plastic bloomers. I picked them up. "Jesus Christ, what the hell is this?" They were lined with some kind of towelling, like pants for people with incontinence.

"That's what we all have to wear, I know they're hideous, but it's all or nothing. They won't give a shit if you don't wear them, but their rules say if you won't wear any part of the uniform you go without any of it until you obey the rules, that means freezing to death."

It was like some Gothic nightmare. I pulled on the plastic bloomers, the stiff plastic crackled as I handled them. "Why these panties, Olivia, what's their thinking?"

"I guess it's to humiliate us as much as anything. They say that if you are caned and it bleeds, it will stop you getting blood everywhere when you sit down."

"What? You are joking, tell me you are."

She turned around and pulled down her plastic panties and lifted her short tartan Academy skirt. Her bottom was striped with dozens of scars. She pulled her bloomers back up and smoothed down her skirt.

"Satisfied? No, I'm not joking. This is a very serious place, be very ,very careful if you're thinking about trying to buck the system."

"Yeah, I hear you."

I put on the rest of the uniform, dark red tartan miniskirt like Olivia's, a pale blue cotton blouse, white knee socks and a pair of vile looking shoes, black, heavy Oxfords with thick soles that fastened with laces. She laughed. "Not very sexy, are they?"

"No they are not. Where's the rest of it then, the Academy blazer?"

"What blazer? What you're wearing is what you've got, that's it."

"But it's so cold in here, don't we get any kind of a jacket?"

She pointed at my yellow rubber slicker. "That's it, that's what you get."

It just got worse and worse. As I moved the plastic of my panties crackled. She noticed my annoyance.

"Yeah, don't worry, when you've had them on for a while the plastic warms up and they don't crackle so much."

I couldn't think of an answer to that. The key rattled in the lock and Murdoch and Nurse Bowles came back into the room. Murdoch looked at me with some satisfaction. "

"Well done, Abbey, I'm pleased to see you've behaved. Both of you come with me."

I saw the nurse pick up my jeans, t-shirt, shoes and underwear.

"Hey, leave my stuff alone, I'll take it with me to my room."

"Girls don't have any of their own clothes in The Academy, Abbey, your clothes will be put in storage and you can have them back when you leave," she said coldly.

I was raging with the indignities and miseries I was being forced to suffer in this stupid place, wearing these crappy clothes and now they were taking my own stuff away. "No way, that's theft, you give me my things right away, lady. I'll call the fucking law."

Murdoch took hold of my arm. "Nurse Bowles has told you the rule, Abbey. I will also tell you that swearing is not allowed, any kind of foul language will be punished."

"Fuck you, arsehole, I don't care, give me my clothes back."

Behind me I could hear Olivia telling me to let it go, to shut up, but I couldn't stop now, I was raging with anger and frustration.

"It's the last time, lady, give me my clothes," I shouted.

"We'll take her to punishment, Nurse Bowles. She's been warned."

He took my other arm, the nurse already had hold of one arm and they pulled me out of the room, I was shouting, swearing and screaming. They marched along the corridor, an assembly bell was ringing and girls dressed identically to me were pouring out of rooms and running along the corridor ahead of us. We arrived in a large hall and I was taken up the stairs to the stage. On the stage was a vaulting horse, they flung me over the horse and while Murdoch held me down Nurse Bowles fastened straps to my wrists and ankles, so that I was spread-eagled. I felt my plastic panties coming down and the cold air on my bare ass. I had gone silent with shock since they strapped me down but now I started to panic and scream. The nurse was ready for me and fastened a gag over my face, a ball pushed inside my mouth and the device was fastened tightly with straps around the back of my head. I looked up and to my horror saw the rest of the girls, there must have been about eighty of them, watching me with fascinated concentration. I tried to shout out but all I managed was a gurgle.

"This new girl has broken the rules, she has been disobedient and even used foul language at the staff," I heard Murdoch telling them. Do you all know the punishment for bad behaviour?"

"Yes, Mr Murdoch," eighty voices said in unison. My flesh crawled, they sounded like robots.

"Very well. Because she is new she will only get fifteen strokes of the cane. Remember, for each future infringement of the rules the punishment doubles."

He walked behind me then, I heard a rustle of clothing as he ran forward and then the world erupted in pain as the first stroke slashed down on my bare ass. I was trying to scream, but knew that I was only making a quiet gurgle, almost like a lunatic. My ass was on fire, I couldn't stand it, but it made no difference what I could stand, there was another rush of feet behind me and he whacked me again. It was like an electric shock running through me, I'd never known pain like it. Yet again, the rush of feet and that red hot searing pain. I thought I was going to die. I looked up and saw the girls staring at me curiously. Whack, another blow, my eyes filled with tears and my whole body shook with sobs. Whack, another one and I knew what sheer terror felt like, not again, oh not again, I prayed inside, but whack, it came again and I shivered with terrified agony, the strokes came thick and fast then, blurring into a long, hot session of pure agony. I heard someone say, "That's fifteen, it's enough for now. Thirty next time, we'll see how she likes that."

My gag was removed and my wrists and ankles unstrapped.

"Pull up your panties, girl," Nurse Bowles said coldly.

I quickly pulled up the cold plastic bloomers. As the material touched my ass the pain knifed through me again. I smoothed my skirt down and waited to see what would happen next.

"Your punishment has ended for now, Abbey," the

nurse said. "You must thank Mr Murdoch, that's how it's done here. Unless you want the next stage in your punishment, that's thirty strokes of the cane."

I shuddered with terror. "Thank you, Mr Murdoch," I said quietly. Surely this had to be an illusion, I was getting out of this madhouse, the first moment I got a chance.

"Very well, behave yourself and you won't need to go through it again. Nurse Bowles, she's had a harsh introduction to Academy life, she can have an early night to bed."

"Come with me," the nurse said. I followed her, meekly this time, I truly was frightened by the violence of this place. She led me upstairs to a dormitory, there was a row of six beds either side of the long room.

"Use the bathroom now, Abbey, before you go to bed. Then get undressed, just leave your panties and bra on."

"Ok, I will," I said. Anything to keep these fuckers away from me. I went to pee and then reported back to the nurse. She handed me a long, coarse cotton nightie that buttoned at the throat, long sleeved and full length to my ankles and indicated my bed, the covers already pulled aside.

"Get in, Abbey, and lie on your stomach."

I did as she said, but as I lay down I felt her fastening straps over me and realised that I was being fastened into a harness to stop me getting out of bed, like they used to use on babies. She pulled the covers over me and left, saying goodnight as she shut the door. I lay there seething with rage and frustration, my ass was on fire, my mind was in agony, this was unbelievable. How could my parents have imprisoned me in a place like this for three whole months, I had never felt so frightened and alone in my life.

## CHAPTER THREE

About an hour later the light in the dormitory came on and the girls that slept here came in, together with Nurse Bowles and another woman, I could hear them talking but couldn't twist my head to see who the new arrival was. I could see the girls either side of me getting undressed in silence. They put on their long nightdresses like mine and then lay on their stomachs on their beds. The nurse and the other woman went to each in turn and fastened their harnesses, the girls didn't object or make any effort to stop them. The women finally finished imprisoning the last girl in her harness and left the room, turning out the light. I twisted my head and called out to the girl to the right of my bed.

"Hey, I'm Abbey, who are you?"

"I'm Zoe Miller, are you the new girl who was punished today?"

I told her yeah, that was me. She sympathized. "Yeah, we all felt that one, he really gave it to you, that sadistic bastard."

"Zoe, pardon me if I seem stupid, but what the hell's going on here? Are you always locked into these harnesses to sleep in?"

"Oh yes, that's the least of our problems, yes, every night, it's to make sure we don't get up to anything they don't like."

"Like escaping, you mean?"

She laughed. "You can forget that, this place is like Devil's Island. No-one escapes."

I thought about that for a moment. "Surely someone must have got off the island, I thought the girls were all here because they were tougher and more rebellious?"

"You've got that right, I guess we've all been pretty wild before our parents sent us here," Zoe continued. "But no, there haven't been any cases that I know of where a girl has got away. We knuckle down and behave and when our term time is up we go home."

"Well fuck'em," I said. "There's no way I'm going to just sit back and let them get away with this."

She laughed. "I hope you'll think again before you do anything stupid, you'll spend a lot of time with a very sore ass. You wait until tomorrow when you see at least a couple of girls standing in class because their backsides are too sore to sit down."

"Christ, are you serious?"

"Yes, I am," she replied. "Take my advice, keep quiet and keep your head down."

I mulled that over in my mind, the trouble was that it just wasn't me. I didn't ever accept the status quo, it wasn't in my nature.

"Zoe, you still awake?"

"Yes."

"Who do we call to be released when we need to go for a pee or something?"

She was quiet for a moment. Then she said, "Nobody. We're all strapped here until they let us out in the morning."

"Yeah, but surely if we're desperate and need to go."

"We're here until morning."

"But what if we really have to go," I persisted.

"Then you do it in your panties, you wet yourself," she said shortly.

Oh my God, this was insane.

"I know it's not easy," she continued. "But this is the way things are, we've all been chucked out of more than one school, The Academy is the last resort. Chill out, do your time and get out of here and make sure you never come back. That's the only way."

I awoke in the early morning, stiff from being confined in the awful harness. There was a definite smell of ammonia in the room, clearly not every girl had been able to wait to go to the bathroom. I was desperate, my bladder bursting, but I resolved to hang on before suffering that ultimate indignity. As the light shone through the drapes, one by one the other girls awoke. There was little chatter or conversation, they were all subdued. Eventually, the door opened and Nurse Bowles came into the room with the other woman. I gathered she was Amanda Drew, she helped out the nurse with a variety of housekeeping and other functions. They started to release us and with a sigh of relief my harness was unlocked and I got up stiffly from the bed. I rushed to the bathroom and even then had to wait five minutes, there was a queue of red-faced girls, desperate to go. Afterwards I followed Zoe, my friend from the next bed, to the shower room. I ran a shower, it was freezing cold.

"How do we get the hot water running, Zoe?"

She laughed "Hot water? You must be joking. There is no hot water, not for anything. We wash and shower in cold water, summer and winter."

Furious, I stepped into the shower and almost died of shock as the icy water cascaded down over my body, but I washed quickly and got out and dried off. We went back to the dormitory and got dressed, there were clean plastic panties in a small chest next to my bed, other than that I had to put on the previous days clothes, bra, blouse, skirt and socks. When Zoe was ready we went down for breakfast.

The food was served in the assembly hall, the stage

with its vaulting horse a stark and terrible reminder of what happened to girls who didn't behave.

"We're not allowed to talk during breakfast," Zoe whispered. "They punish any talking or noise with a whacking, so don't even think about it."

A hard faced woman of about middle age, maybe forty years old stormed up to us. "Zoe, were you talking, what do you think you're doing?"

My friend went white, she was visibly trembling. "I was just explaining the rules about talking to the new girl, Mrs Rogers."

"You know the rules, no talking for any reason. Up to the stage."

To my astonishment, Zoe went quietly with her, not even a protest. While we all watched she was led to the vaulting horse, strapped down with her panties around her ankles and Mrs Rogers took out the cane.

"This girl has broken the rules by talking during breakfast, it's the second offence this month so she gets thirty strokes. This should be a warning to all of you, be absolutely silent during breakfast or you'll be punished."

Thirty strokes! I could hardly believe it, she'd only been whispering. Mrs Rogers walked to the back of the stage and then ran forward and caned her hard on the ass. I saw Zoe's face screw up in agony.

It reminded me of the spanking I had endured the day before, I recalled the terrible pain and mental anguish and felt so sorry for her. The blows rained down, each one echoed across the hall with a loud 'whack' as it slapped down on her bare ass. She was sobbing now, crying, then her cries turned to shrieks and screams as the number of blows came to twenty. Mrs Rogers paused, put the cane down and fitted the gag on her, the one they'd used on me, reducing her shouts to a muffled gurgle. Then the caning went on, relentlessly and she sobbed in silence, the tears pouring from her eyes. I felt the tension in the room ease when the caning ended and she was released. In a trembling voice she said, "Thank you for caning me, Mrs Rogers," and then left the stage. She came back to our table where her breakfast, the same as we all had, thick, unappetizing porridge, had congealed and gone cold. She didn't sit down but stood to eat it. I had finished mine and I sat looking around me, but not daring to say anything. Finally a bell rang and all the girls got up, I followed them with Zoe and we went to our classroom. I sat behind a desk, Zoe stood. I recalled what she had said about girls standing up, there were two others who obviously had been thrashed recently, they were standing too. My ass was sore, but thankfully not that sore.

No-one spoke, I had no need to ask why not. Eventually, a teacher came into the classroom. He introduced himself as Mr Andrews.

"Today we will be looking at the question of English history under the Tudors."

He smiled at us, not a pleasant smile. He looked like a total pervert, flabby, greasy, a sneering smile on his lips, I pictured him as one of the Tudor flunkeys, plotting and scheming in King Henry the Eight's court. He would have been perfectly in character.

"You three girls, why are you standing up?"

"Sir, we were caned, it's too sore to sit down," Zoe said.

"Hmm, I don't like you standing up in my class, it makes the room look untidy. Sit down, all of you. If it hurts, it serves you right for misbehaving."

I could see Zoe's eyes fill with tears, she sat down and winced, doing her best to sit on the very edge of the chair and holding her weight with her hands on the desk. At first Mr Andrews ignored her plight and carried on with the lesson, but I noticed hi sneaking glances at her painful discomfort, enjoying every second of it. By the end of the session, Zoe was shaking and perspiring with the effort of keeping most of her weight off her sore bottom, tears pouring down her face. I put my arm around her and took some of her weight, helping her up as the teacher left the classroom. The lesson had lasted an hour and a half, I'd never known one so long.

Several girls started speaking, I gathered it was at last safe to do so.

"Zoe, I'm sorry you got into trouble for warning me, that was a rotten thing to happen to you."

She shrugged. "I should have known what to expect,

God knows we've all been warned and thrashed enough to know. It's not your fault."

We followed the rest of the girls through to a new classroom, a music room where we had to listen to a boring talk about the finer rudiments of classical music of the Renaissance period. As if anyone gave a shit. At least Zoe and the other two girls were allowed to stand, so her ass was spared another session of tortured sitting. At last it was lunchtime and we went to the hall, the vaulting horse still standing on the stage, threatening us all, a sober reminder to behave. They were wasting their time with me, I only saw it as just another challenge in a long series of life's challenges. Did they honestly think that their stupid strict regime was going to make any difference to the way I behaved? Yes, of course they did think that, but they'd be wrong and all of their efforts and my parents wasted money would be for nothing. I fully intended to play the game for now and keep looking for ways to disrupt this perverted lunatic asylum.

Food was a kind of strew with stringy, tough meat, quite disgusting. Pudding was typical of The Academy meals too, stodgy sponge with custard. Unbelievable.

"We're supposed to go out and walk around after lunch, get some fresh air," Zoe said to me. She'd eaten her food standing up.

"No thanks, I want to look around this place and see where everything is."

"Abbey," she smiled. "You don't get it do you? We have to go out and walk around after lunch, it's not optional, you know. Unless of course you want the alternative?"

She looked at the empty vaulting horse on the stage. I shuddered. "Ok, maybe we'll go for a walk."

She grinned through her pain. "Let's go up and get our coats."

"What for? I don't want to wear that horrible yellow waterproof. Besides, the weather may be nice outside."

She shook her head. "Two things, Abbey. Firstly, the weather here is never, ever nice. It's almost always wet, cold and miserable. Secondly, the rule is that we have to wear the yellow coats whenever we go outside, no matter what the weather. Wearing them means they have to be fastened to the neck with the hood over your head and tied securely under the chin. I don't need to tell you the penalty for getting it wrong."

"Shit, what a fucking hellhole," I snarled.

Zoe looked around, alarmed. "For God's sake, Abbey, cut out the swearing, they'll thrash you for that."

I shook my head. What could I get away with here? I'd find something.

## CHAPTER FOUR

We walked up to the dormitory and took our yellow slickers off the pegs beside our beds. I pulled mine on, it was cold and clammy, but I zipped it up to the throat, put the hood over my head and tied the strings tightly under my chin. Zoe did the same and we walked down the stairs and out into the cold, damp Scottish climate.

"What's the deal with these yellow macs?" I asked her.

She laughed. "Look ahead, what do you see?"

There were thirty or forty girls in view, bright yellow figures walking along the paths across the small island.

"Yeah, I get it. No way to hide when you're covered in bright yellow from the head down, is that it?"

"You've got it. We stand out like beacons."

We walked around like prisoners in an exercise yard, which is more or less what we were. We were like robots, we looked alike, moved alike, and were even programmed to do or not do exactly the same things. I resolved there and then that whatever it took, I was going to make greater efforts to get out of this, not matter what it took.

"Have you ever thought about getting off the island and going home?" I asked Zoe.

She smiled. "Every day, I hate it here. My parents enrolled me for twelve months, I've done five months already and I can't wait to get home. Trouble is, I was pretty bad, they were really pissed off with me."

I thought about my own behaviour, it hadn't been that bad. "What did you do, what sort of stuff?"

"I was going out every night, drinking, guys, you know the routine, drugs too, the headmistress found out and gave me a load of detentions so I set fire to her car. I was expelled and sent here. What about you?"

I shrugged. "I don't think I did any real damage like you did, I just fucked around, didn't take any shit from the teachers, swore at them when I felt like it. Have you been spanked very often here?"

Zoe made a face. "Yeah, at least twice a month, if I don't do anything bad the new month starts soon and I go back to fifteen strokes of the cane. Otherwise it's sixty, they double up every time."

"Jesus Christ, how can you take as many as sixty, has it ever happened?"

I could see her face pale as she remembered. "Yep, it did happen once. Fifteen strokes, then thirty, then sixty, just before the end of the month. It was terrible, Abbey really awful, I couldn't sit down for a week."

"So how about getting away from here? It doesn't make any difference, does it, the threat of punishment, or do you think it does?"

She was thoughtful for a moment. "I guess it does for some of the girls, you must have noticed already. We're all of us pretty bad, but most of them here are already totally cowed, they toe the line and behave. Until they leave, anyway."

"What about you," I persisted. "Has it made any difference to you?"

"Oh yes, it won't be the car that gets torched next time, it'll be the whole fucking place."

I was still laughing when we got back to Academy for the afternoon's lessons. We'd discussed a couple of ideas for getting off the island, there'd be time to take it further when I had a better idea of where everything was. Like a boat, without that we'd no chance. The headmaster was waiting at the door as all of us girls filed in.

"Abbey, Zoe, how was your walk, are you ready to do some work now?"

"Not really, no," I said automatically. I guess on my first day here I wasn't programmed like some of these girls.

"Really, why is that then?" he asked with a smirk on his face.

"Because I don't like this fucking place, that's why."

Zoe was trying to pull me away. "No, Abbey, don't do this, shut up."

I shrugged her arm off, I suppose all of my rage and frustration boiled over.

"Look, my friend, you may think that you can knock my confidence with your stupid threats but I'm not having any of it, I've got rights, you know, so fuck you and fuck your piece of shit Academy."

"Abbey leave it out, come to class now," Zoe pleaded.

Murdoch rounded on her. "Zoe, get to your class. What is your next punishment, is it sixty?"

She nodded.

"Then I suggest you go now."

She lowered her head meekly and walked away.

"You'd better come with me, Abbey, you don't seem to have learned your lesson, do you?"

I realised then that I'd gone too far, my ass still hurt from the previous beating I'd had.

"Ok, look, I'm sorry I swore, I'm just not used to being here."

He laughed out loud. "No, you're not," he replied. "But don't worry, we'll soon take care of that."

"Where are we going?"

"We'll go and see Nurse Bowles and sort you out there."

We arrived at the nurse's room and he pushed straight in, dragging me after him by the arm. The nurse and her assistant, Amanda Drew, were attending to a girl who was lying naked on the examination couch, her legs up in stirrups, her cunt on view for everyone to see. The women whirled around. "Headmaster, we were just completing an examination," the Nurse said.

Murdoch just stood looking curiously at the girl's vagina, as if it was a piece of Academy equipment.

"No problem, Nurse, you finish off, we'll just stand here and wait."

The girl on the table had her eyes shut, her face was flushed red but she was too terrified to protest. While he stood watching the nurses took swabs and applied cream to her cunt, the nurse put a surgical rubber glove on her hand and pushed it deeply inside her hole. I sensed the headmaster shifting and fidgeting as he watched closely. I could bet he had a hard on. It was on the tip of my tongue to call him a fucking pervert and tell him to leave the girl alone, but I was in enough trouble, I hadn't any idea why he'd brought me here but I suspected it wasn't for anything pleasant.

Eventually the examination was finished and the girl was allowed off the table and she pulled up her plastic panties and left the room, I nodded to her as she went past, hot and uncomfortable after the unwelcome intrusion.

"I want her on the table, Nurse Bowles, face down, feet in the stirrups, she is to be punished for bad language."

Oh fuck, I didn't need this. "Look, it wasn't anything much, can't you forget it," I said hastily.

"What? Of course I can't forget it, you were warned, weren't you?"

I started to back out of the room but he grabbed me, I was still wearing my yellow rubber mac with the hood up, he scooped up the skirts of the coat and hoisted them over my head so that I was powerless. Then he threw me on the table and I felt my panties being pulled down and my feet hoisted into the stirrups. I kept struggling to get away, but someone fastened a belt over my body that held me to the table and I was powerless. With the skirts of the coat over my hooded head I couldn't hear much, but I gathered that they were discussing how many strokes to give me. Faintly, I heard the word thirty and I shuddered, no, I remembered the first spanking, fifteen terrible, agonising strokes, I couldn't manage thirty. The first stroke hit me, I heard it faintly but the pain was terrible on my injured rear, searing through me like a bolt of electricity.

I realized I was screaming, shouting, pleading, but it was like being trapped in a machine, my head enclosed in the waterproof skirts of my mac. Whack, the pain came again, my whole body jerked off the table and came back down with a thump. The blows came thick and fast, smashing into my buttocks, stroke after stroke after stroke, so loud that I could actually hear the meaty sound as they landed. Whack, another hard stroke slashed into me, I was burning now, burning with intense pain. Whack, I was on fire, still screaming for him to stop. Whack, it was as if her was deaf, whack, again, I jerked and writhed, trying to move my rear so that the sorest parts were away from the implacable strokes, but he was an expert. He simply altered the site that he hit with the cane, seeming to hit the same place repeatedly for maximum pain. Eventually I gave up protesting, just lay there with my head in its dark, hooded prison and waited for it to end.

I sensed light as my PVC panties and were pulled back over my legs and my mac pulled down, the punishment had ended. My ankles were still held in the stirrups, I heard Murdoch speaking to the nurse.

"You'd better get the wounds treated, Nurse Bowles. She's a tough one this one, I want her ready for punishment again, I think it will take many sessions before she learns her lesson. I don't want an injured ass saving her from being caned again."

He gripped my head and turned it towards him. I was barely registering what was being said, the pain was so bad I just wanted to pass out.

"Well?" he asked me.

Just in time, I remembered. "Thank you for punishing me, Mr Murdoch."

"Good. Remember, Abbey, the next time it will be sixty strokes, let me assure you that it would sting."

I shivered. Sixty strokes, my God, I couldn't stand that, I'd die. I'd have to behave, have to control my temper, my distaste for authority. I couldn't take any more.

"Have you got the video tape, Nurse Bowles, I'll take it with me?"

I saw her go to a video camera that I hadn't noticed before and extract a digital tape and hand it to him. So he'd even had my spanking recorded, oh my God, it was so sick. I had visions of my bare ass being spanked and broadcast on the Internet. Or was it only for his own pleasure, the sick bastard?

"Abbey, I want you to keep your yellow waterproof coat on, fastened and the hood up at all times, inside and outside the Academy, until further notice."

"Why?" I asked him, curious at such an odd request.

"I sometimes insist on that with girls who I think will cause trouble, it marks you out so that I can keep an eye on you. Make sure you do it, how many strokes are you due the next time?"

"Sixty, Mr Murdoch."

"Very well, I suggest you behave and do as you're told."

He left the infirmary and the nurse gave me some cream for my ass.

"You've got a lot of bruising there," Nurse Bowles said. "You won't be able to sit properly for a couple of days. Some of your cuts have bled a little, I've put dressings on them. Be very careful not to damage them."

Jesus Christ, he'd drawn blood. What kind of a sadist was he?

"Abbey, listen to me," the nurse said. "You're new here, and you seem to want to challenge authority. You must behave, if you took a beating of sixty strokes right now, it would damage you very, very badly, you wouldn't be able to sit for a fortnight. For your own good, do as you're told and behave."

"Yes, Nurse Bowles," I said. It was true, I did intend to do my best to behave, as far as they would see. But I was already plotting revenge.

I got off the table and straightened the yellow waterproof that cocooned me from head to calf. I winced as my weight came onto my hips, to say they hurt was an understatement. A fire still swept through my lower regions and despite all of my resolution to plot revenge, the only thing uppermost in my mind at that moment was to behave, to obey and not to get into any more trouble. I walked, or limped out of the door and pulled it closed. Just before it shut, I heard one of the women say, "I don't think it's right that the headmaster should use those films of the girls being spanked for his own amusement."

Oh yes, so that was how it went. How could I use that information to my advantage? As I limped away I passed the door to the headmaster's office. I walked past a few yards and his door opened, I quickly moved into an open classroom and looked around. Murdoch came out and turned and walked away from me in the opposite direction. I just had to know what was going on here, The

Academy was so twisted and perverted in the excessive punishmentments that they inflicted on girls, but it was more than that, it was the joy that they seemed to take in the punishments. All I needed was some proof that he was secretly watching spanking videos to be sent to the authorities to get his comeuppance, once and for all.

I weighed up in my mind whether to go and look over his office. Wearing the hooded yellow waterproof made me a visible target for anyone to see, it was a signal that the wearer was a troublemaker, which was of course why they made us wear them indoors. If I got caught, I would be in line for sixty strokes of the cane, I couldn't take that, it could kill me, but if I didn't try, I'd never get out of here and expose these perverts for what they were, at the very least my parents needed to know what their daughter was suffering. Then it came to me, if I was going to take the risk, I should just take the mac off, if they caught me I was done for anyway. I checked both ways, it was clear, quickly I unfastened the hood, pulled it down, unzipped the front of the coat and took it off and stuffed under my arm. It was now or never, I ran along to the office, looked inside the door and found it empty, then I slipped in. Initially it looked like any head teachers office, bookshelves, a desk cluttered with files and papers, TV with DVD player, filing cabinet. Filing cabinet, that was a possibility. I opened the top drawer, nothing. The middle drawer, just a load of files and paper. The bottom drawer was stiff at first, but I pulled hard and it came open. Bingo! Dozens of home-made DVDs, all neatly labelled. The DVD at the top had Zoe Miller's name on, I took it out and slipped the disk in the DVD player, pressed play and turned on the television. The screen came to life and there was Zoe, two cameras in split screen, one zoomed in on her agonized, tortured face, the other showing her ass and the cane as it rose and fell on her ass, Murdoch running across the stage each time and bringing the cane down on her with his full force. I gasped, it was pure porn, one of the worst, most disgusting films I'd ever seen. So our headmaster got off on watching re-runs of girls in pain being thrashed until they screamed in the worst possible agony. The evidence was all here in the office. All I needed was to find a way of making what he was doing public.

"If you'd come in my office, Miss West, I'll sign your forms for you," I heard Murdoch say outside the office.

Christ, he was back. I looked around quickly, there was a door behind his desk, I ran to it, opened it and went into a large walk in closet, a small storeroom.

## CHAPTER FIVE

I was just in time, the door opened and Murdoch and the young female teacher came into the office. As they talked I looked around the small storeroom, on the shelves were television monitors, I wondered what the hell he was up to in here. As I watched, a light came on one monitor and I was looking at the Academy stage where the spankings took place. Another showed the infirmary, Nurse Bowles was attending to a girl I hadn't seen before, the camera was positioned in such a way that it looked straight at her vagina, clearly he could record any of that activity at any time.

There were four other TV monitors there, all switched off, I really didn't want to know where those cameras were positioned, I'd seen enough. I waited for them to finish what they were doing in the office so that I could get out, but there was no sign of anyone moving away. I put my ear to the door and was able to make out the voices.

"Headmaster, while we are having this discussion in private, I wanted to express my concern that your corporal punishment is going too far, I feel that the girls are being hurt too much."

"Is that so, Miss West," Murdoch replied. "Have you ever been punished like that, severely caned?"

There was a silence. Then she replied in a shocked voice. "Well, no, Headmaster, I have not."

"Then perhaps you should know what it feels like, Miss West. As it happens, I have a cane here in my office, you'd better lean over the chair and take down your panties."

Her voice rose to an astonished shout of protest. "I'll do no such thing, Mr Murdoch, this is outrageous."

"Miss West, believe me, you will do it, I regard it as essential that you understand what the girls are going through, otherwise you're no use to me here. I gather it's not easy to get a job these days, especially when your qualifications are so poor?"

She murmured something, I didn't catch what it was. There was silence for a moment then I heard the familiar whack of the cane, a scream from the woman, then another whack. She was protesting to him, but the cane whacked down again and again, now her voice was different, I wondered why she was putting up with it. Her voice had gone hoarse, something about it was familiar and I suddenly realize that it was lust, sexual arousal. They were both turned on by the caning, she was obviously loving it. I heard the sound of heavy breathing, moans and panting. I decided to take the chance and peeked out of the door. The teacher was bent over the chair, her panties on the floor. Murdoch was screwing her, taking her from behind and they were both putting a lot of effort into it and having a lot of fun. They grunted and moaned, she was wailing softly to him, "Julian, oh that's so good, oh God, fuck me harder, Jesus, it's so good."

He did his best to give her what she wanted, I could see, redoubling his efforts, after a few minutes their arousal peaked and the hoarse pants crescendoed, the room was filled with the moaning and shrieking of sexual orgasm. Then he pulled out of her and I saw the new, red stripes on her bum. Well, well. I wondered was he recording that for his little collection. But I had an important mission on my hands and that was to get out of here as fast as possible without being seen.

I decided to play it safe and I quietly slipped on my yellow waterproof, pulled the hood over my head, fastened my zip and strings under my chin and waited for an opportunity. Please, go to the bathroom, I willed them silently. Sure enough, Murdoch said to her, "Miss West, perhaps we should go and clean up?"

She pulled up her panties and smiled at him. "Yes, we should, I hope we'll be doing that again soon, Julian."

"No problems with the spanking any more, Amy?"

"No, Julian, no problems at all. You keep on doing it and I'll be with you all the way, you have my unqualified support."

"Fair enough, let's get cleaned up. Don't forget it's Mr Murdoch outside of the privacy of this office.

They left the room and I took the opportunity to slip out. I was just in time for the evening meal and I made sure that I sat next to Zoe. In any case, no-one else wanted to sit near me, the yellow waterproof worn indoors meant troublemaker and these girls had all felt the agony of repeated canings, they gave me a wide berth. Afterwards I told her what I'd seen.

She was not totally astonished when I told her what I'd found.

"The bastard should be arrested, Abbey. The problem is how can we tell anyone outside the island what is going on here? We've got no way of speaking to anyone, no access to a telephone, no Internet, no postal service, nothing."

"That's true, except that there has to be some kind of communication, if someone falls ill or something. They surely need to keep in touch with prospective customers, there has to communication somewhere. Maybe that's our best chance, to find out where their phone is or maybe their Internet connection."

Then a thought occurred to me. "Zoe, supposing he's selling this stuff, there's a huge market on the Internet for porn and young women being spanked on graphic videos would probably make a fortune for Murdoch."

She nodded. "It makes sense, he's sitting on a gold mine here if he markets it right, while we're just sitting on our sore asses. It's the perfect scam. We're going to need some solid proof though, to make it stick."

"Right, so we need to keep out of trouble for now and find out more about his scheme," I said determinedly.

"Do we? Do we really need to keep out of trouble?"

I looked at her, amazed. "Well shit, yeah, we've both just been caned, surely you don't want any more?"

"No, of course not. But we're both in line for a major caning if we do something badly wrong, how would our asses look to the authorities after sixty strokes of the cane? It could completely cook his goose, assault charges as the very least."

I shook my head. "No, that's going too far. What we've suffered already and the porn videos would be enough, believe me."

As she said it I was reminded of the pain, the agony of the caning, thirty terrible strokes. I thought about what I had overheard in the headmaster's office, caning Amy West as a preliminary to sex. And I became moist, to my shame I felt aroused at the thought of a caning followed by sex. It was astonishing, I felt guilty just to feel that way. Zoe was looking at me intently, misreading the signals. "Look," she said. "If you're in a lot of pain I'll take a look at your ass and see if the scars are really bad, you might even be bleeding. You're right, another caning would be too much. Would you like me to do that?"

I hesitated, but only for a moment. "Yes, I would, can we go somewhere quiet?"

"There's no-one in the dormitory at the moment, they don't send us to bed for at least another hour. We could go there."

"Let's go," I replied, a little too eagerly.

In the dormitory I stripped off my yellow waterproof and took off my plastic panties. As I lay on my bed Zoe pulled up my skirt and inspected my rear. She touched one of my wounds and I jumped, but even as I did I felt my vagina becoming moist with the beginnings of arousal.

"Did I hurt you?" she said anxiously.

"No, no, please carry on, it's very soothing, it's nice.

She understood what I wanted immediately, her hands started to stroke my rear, getting nearer and nearer to my vagina. Then she felt inside my labia, touched the moistness and realized how desperate I was. She moved her fingers towards my clit and I jerked as if I'd been hit with Mr Murdoch's strongest blow. But this was no painful punishment, it was the soothing, sensual touch of a sympathetic soul. A lover? I wasn't sure, after all, although I'd spent years at girl's boarding schools and knew that lesbian sex was not necessarily wrong, I'd always been uncomfortable with it. But here in this harsh, unforgiving place there were few if any chances for any kind of human warmth or touch. Whatever was being offered to me, I wanted it.

She started to gently rub my clit and I put my arm behind me and held her to me. She put two fingers inside my hole and started to push in and out, keeping up the pressure on my clit, I writhed and groaned with the pleasure of her touch. There was something missing, something that I wanted to ask her for but felt too embarrassed to mention. But my need overcame me, I had to have more.

"Zoe, would you do something else for me?"

"Of course I will, you want me to spank you, don't you?"

"Yeah, I'm sorry, it's just that after overhearing Murdoch and Amy West doing it, I feel so hot. Is that bad, in a place like this where caning is so horrible and cruel?"

She giggled. "Let me tell you my secret, Abbey. When the caning gets really bad and it hurts so much, I have a mental fucking session, I think of my favourite fantasy and while that sick bastard is whacking me, I pretend that it's some gorgeous guy who's doing it to me and then fucking me. I make all the agonized noises but really I'm not feeling the pain so much as my lover's cock, ramming in and out of my cunt. So leave it to me, my darling, I'll make it good for you."

"Thank you, Zoe."

I lay back and shut my eyes, waiting for what was to

come. She slapped me, gently, it stung a little but I felt my body arching up to meet the blow, then she hit me again slightly harder. My body yearned for the touch of her hand, spanking me on the bottom, my cunt was on fire now as she continued playing with my clit and my hole, the ecstasy was slowly enveloping me and starting to take me away from this stark, dreadful place. She spanked me harder.

"Do you want me to keep going, make it harder?" she asked me.

"Yes please, do it," I begged her.

Then her hand came down hard on my rear and it scorched through me, the shockwaves from the blow meeting the pleasure waves of her hand in my cunt and combining to make something I wouldn't have thought possible, a kind of pleasure and pain combination like sweet and sour sauce. I smiled inside at the absurd analogy, but it was true, the sweetness of her masturbating me worked with the sour pain of the spanking to make the experience unique. David, my previous lover had fucked me several times but it was never like this. All of a sudden I was on fire, my hips pushing up to meet both her hands, she knew what I wanted. One hand stroked harder, deeper while the other slapped harder and harder, almost as hard as Murdoch had hurt me with the cane, but this time it was arousing, erotic and far from wanting it to stop I wanted it to last forever.

She spanked me repeatedly and I got hotter and hotter, my mind went completely blank, all I could think of was the repeated stroking and spanking, for me the rest of the world had ceased to exist. I burned hotter and hotter, then finally I couldn't wait any longer and I came to a massive climax, I gripped Zoe to me as hard as I could and held her while she pushed her fingers inside of me and stroked and spanked to the very end. I lay back exhausted.

"Zoe, that was fantastic, I feel light headed. What can I do for you?"

She put her head down close to mine. "I want you to eat me, go down on me, lick me and keep licking until I come."

The thought of going down on her, sucking her luscious, exotic cunt was too much for me, I felt myself becoming aroused just by the thought of licking her. I pushed her onto the bed where she lay on her back, removed her PVC panties and pushed her knees apart. Then I buried my head between them and sunk my mouth into the dark, damp warmth of her cunt, using my tongue to lick her clit and suck her at the same time. I put my hands around her body, I so wanted her erotic warmth close to me and once more lost myself to the pleasure of having sex with my new partner.

## CHAPTER SIX

Zoe climaxed, a wonderful, powerful orgasm that threatened to shake the foundations of the Academy, I was worried in case anyone passing the dormitory overheard, but we were safe. Afterwards, we lay in each other's arms, happy in our shared warmth and the afterglow of sex. We heard the sound of girl's voices coming towards us, suddenly she leapt up, alarmed.

"Abbey, your mac!"

"What? What about it?"

"You're supposed to have it on at all times inside the Academy."

Oh, Christ, what a nuisance. I put the yellow rubber coat on, zipped it up and tied the hood. Then we sat chatting quietly and innocently as the girls started to file in to get ready for bed. One by one they went to the bathroom and then stripped off and put on their coarse nightdresses and lay down ready to be strapped in, what docile creatures they were, I thought. How cowed by the brutal thrashings administered in the Academy. I lost myself in planning how to bring them to their just desserts and hardly noticed as Nurse Bowles came marching into the room with her assistant Amanda Drew. They came straight over to me.

"Lie down, Abbey, it's time for you to be strapped in."

I looked at them aghast. "Hey, I haven't even had time to undress or use the bathroom, would you do someone else first and let me have a few minutes?"

Her look was hard and cold, she reminded me of Nurse Ratched from the movie One Flew Over The Cuckoo's Nest.

"No second chances, those are the rules at this Academy and you must obey them. Lie down unless you want the next level of punishment."

I hadn't even had time to remove the rubber mac that I was encased in. For a moment I was tempted to tell them to go fuck themselves and take the consequences, after all, we had discussed it. But I was frightened, terrified of that amount of pain. I lay down in my mac and they fastened my harness, then went around and strapped in the other girls. I lay there, covered in yellow rubber, even my head was covered by the hood, I felt uncomfortable and nauseated, how on earth could I manage do spend a night like this, and how could I manage to get through a night without going to the bathroom. Already, my bladder was reminding me that I needed to go. The lights went out and I lay there for hour after hour, terrified at what might happen, trying to do everything possible not to have to urinate until I was released in the morning. I tried to move my hands around to undo my straps, but they were designed for restraint and I had to give it up as a bad job. I tried thinking of other things, so that I wouldn't be totally focused on urinating, but in the end it was all a waste of time, I couldn't manage to last for the whole night. Feeling terrified, ashamed and uncomfortable I had to let my bladder release and I peed myself in my PVC panties, then I had to lay in the pool of urine held trapped by the panties, at first it was warm but it slowly cooled and I was left trapped in a pool of sopping, stinking piss.

In the morning they came to release us. Nurse Bowles could smell it as soon as she came into the room and she walked over to me, a cold smile on her face.

"Did you have a good night, Abbey?" she said. "Comfortable, were you?"

I shaking with rage and humiliation, having to wait for this woman to free me from my disgusting imprisonment, but I knew that I could do nothing to vent that anger for fear that the sixty strokes of the cane that I was threatened with became a reality.

"Yes, thank you, Nurse Bowles," I replied.

"Good, I'm pleased to hear it. But what is that I can smell? Have you wet yourself, dear?"

Her smile broadened. "Yes, Nurse Bowles, I have," I replied.

Her nose crinkled in mock disgust. "Dear me, that is disgusting. As soon as I undo your harness you'd better visit the bathroom and change your underwear, hadn't you? Make sure you wash out your dirty panties and put them to dry, there is a clean pair in your drawer."

"Yes, Nurse Bowles," I went on. She still hadn't released me, I was trembling with embarrassment and discomfort, desperate to get up and clean myself up.

"Abbey, in view of your problem with controlling yourself," she continued. "You'd better wear your yellow waterproof mac every night, you can sleep in it for the next week and see if your problem happens again."

"But Nurse Bowles, you know why it happened, you wouldn't allow me to go to the bathroom last night."

Her eyes lit up. "Are you arguing with me, Abbey?"

My terror surfaced again, the fear of the lashing strokes of the cane. "No, Nurse Bowles."

"I think you need to learn a lesson, my dear. You may sleep in the mac for the next month. Was there anything else before I release you?"

"No, Nurse Bowles."

She released my harness and thankfully I made my way to the bathroom, removed my sopping wet panties and cleaned up as best I could. I washed them out and hung them to dry. Still wearing the yellow mac, I went back to my bedside and took out a clean set of PVC panties and pulled them on. The other girls had been released and gratefully rushed to the bathroom, then got dressed in Academy uniform and went down to breakfast, I followed them down with Zoe.

"Abbey, I don't know how you survived that one," she said. "I thought you were going to smash her face in and throw her through the window."

I laughed. "If it wasn't for the threat of the next spanking I'd have done it too, fucking cow."

Zoe looked uneasy as I swore. I was wearing the bright yellow mac of course, making me a beacon for everyone to watch out for, but there was nobody within earshot. We went to breakfast and ate the inedible slop they served, at least in that respect I guess it was little different to any English boarding school.

"So when do we start?" my friend murmured to me, twisting around to make sure no-one could see her talking.

"It's already started, Zoe. Every spare moment we need to hunt around, after breakfast, after lunch, between classes, after dinner. We need to find their connection to the mainland, telephone, Internet or whatever. Once we've got that we can nail these fuckers once and for all."

"What about the parents of all of these girls, you'd think they'd be up in arms."

I grimaced. "Yeah, you'd think so, but most of them are probably so grateful to have their naughty girls back as docile little lambs, terrified to put a foot wrong in case they're sent back here to be caned repeatedly. No, we need to get them on their using the images for sexual gratification. That and excessive physical abuse, that'll cook them once and for all."

We finished our breakfast and had to report straight to our first class. I had a plan now and I was determined to be the model of a well behaved girl until I had a chance to screw them. I sat at my desk in my yellow mac, properly fastened, hood tied under my chin and worked hard at being polite and studious. They bought it, that was obvious, they smiled and nodded as I attended to my work and answered them with yes sir, no sir, whatever you want sir. We got our first chance after lunch when we had almost an hour to look around the school. I stuck out like a lighthouse in my yellow mac, exactly as they intended, but as most of the other girls were going out of the building to walk around wearing identical macs it wasn't quite so obvious.

We looked in rooms, offices and closets for anything that might contain a telephone line and a computer, but found nothing. Then it struck me.

"Of course, if they have a telephone line, it will come into the building from somewhere outside. Let's take a look around."

As we raced to the door, Zoe suddenly said, "My mac, I have to get it, I can't go out without it."

I nodded. "I'll see you outside, I'm going to look around."

I went outside, as usual it was grey and raining. At least I didn't stand out like a sore thumb, everyone was wearing yellow macs like mine. I walked around the building looking up for anywhere that suggested cables coming into the building. There was only one possibility, a huge satellite dish on the roof with several cables dropping into a room that was just under the eaves, probably an attic room. That was the first place to check. As I was going back into the building I met Zoe coming out in her yellow mac. I told her what I'd seen and led her around to see it for herself.

"It sure looks like a possibility," she said. "When are we going up to check that room?"

"After dinner, it'll be dark outside then and there aren't many people moving around the building, we can go up and check it out."

She nodded and we turned around and went back inside. She took off her mac and returned it to the dormitory, I of course had to keep mine on. We attended the afternoon lessons, had dinner and finally had a clear space of time to go and check out the room where the satellite cables disappeared into. We crept up the stairs, it was on the fourth floor and found a series of doors, some locked and three of them open. As we walked along one of the doors opened and we ducked back through one of the unlocked doors into an empty room. We flattened against the wall where we couldn't be seen. I heard Murdoch's voice.

"We need to get those latest video clips edited and uploaded as soon as possible, you know what these customers are like, they want fresh stuff all the time."

"I'll go back and do some work on them later, headmaster. Don't worry, they'll be ready for tomorrow."

"They'd better be, Erica, there's a lot of money at stake here. You realize how unique this product is? We've got the only setup in Europe that can offer a constant supply of spanking porn, a whole Academy full of naughty girls whose parents are paying us money for the pleasure of having their little darlings spanked and disciplined for us to film them. It's perfect, but only for as long as our clients get the product."

I realized it was one of the teachers, Erica Rogers who was with him. It seemed that she was the technical person who edited the videos into the versions that were peddled on the internet. I thought of the images of myself being caned, especially when my feet were held in the stirrups. Cameras almost sticking up my cunt, it was truly horrific.

We waited for them to go down the stairs, then walked along to the room they had come out of. As expected, it was locked.

"How are we going to get through this door?" Zoe asked me.

I looked at it carefully. Then I smiled. "See that

padlock on the door, the screws have been driven in from the outside. All we need is a screwdriver and we can remove the screws, the door will open and when we've checked inside we put the screws back. Simple."

"That's great, Abbey. Where do we find a screwdriver?"

I knew exactly where. We found our way to the handyman's room, the guy was still in there, working on repairing a wooden chair.

"Hi," Zoe said brightly. I didn't feel very sexy in my yellow mac so I left the chat to her. "We wondered what you did with all of this wood and stuff. You can even repair a broken chair, can you?" she gushed, wide eyed.

At first he looked at us as if we were crazy, but in the end pride got the better of him, it wasn't every day that two young girls came into his workshop and showed interest in what he was doing, even in a girl's academy.

"Yes, it's not too difficult, I take out the broken piece, shape a new piece of wood to fit and glue and screw it in place, here, take a look at this."

He moved aside to let Zoe see what he was doing, I stood next to his tray of tools and saw the screwdriver we needed. It was dead easy, while he was making sure that he leaned against Zoe's tits I put it in the pocket of my waterproof coat. He put his arm around Zoe while he was showing her his work and she nodded and made appropriate noises for a couple of minutes. Abruptly she looked around at me. "Abbey, we need to meet the headmaster, he said he wanted to see us, we'd better go quickly."

She twisted out of his arm and together we made for the door, thanking him as we left the workshop. Fucking creep. Then we went back up to the top floor and started to remove the screws on the padlock fastening. The door swung open.

Inside was a complete computer video editing studio, we could see hard drive lights flashing, a broadband modem was connected to the internet via the satellite link. On the screen a video was playing, presumably streaming out to the internet, showing one of the girls, we didn't recognize her, being thrashed with a cane. Like the other videos, this was split screen, simultaneously showing her rear, her cunt and her ass twitching as the cane lashed down and her face, contorting in agony. Then Zoe checked her watch. "Christ, it's nearly bedtime. We'll have to leave this for now and come back tomorrow, if we're late getting to the dormitory they'll search for us and we'll be in more trouble than I could imagine."

We left the room and I fastened the screws back to the padlock. It looked exactly as we had found it. Then we ran all the way back to the dorm room. As soon as we walked through the door I knew I was in trouble. The girls were all harnessed in for the night and Nurse Bowles was looking at her watch as I arrived, Zoe hung back hoping perhaps she hadn't noticed her missing. All I saw was her joy at being able to persecute me again. Her eyes gleamed with satisfaction.

"You never learn, do you, Abbey. Get yourself straight into bed."

"Nurse, I have to go to the bathroom, I can't take another night like before," I said desperately. I sprinted past her but Amanda Drew put out her foot and tripped me and I went down sprawling on the floor. They picked me up, I was stunned by the fall, and they put me on my bed and fastened my harness.

"Please, no, don't do this to me, let me go to the bathroom, don't humiliate me by making me wet myself again."

"You should have thought of that before," she said sternly, but there was a note of excitement in her voice. "Especially as you'll have a meeting with the headmaster tomorrow for breaking the rules. It's sixty strokes of the cane, isn't it?"

"No," I sobbed. "Please don't do this to me."

I may as well have spoken to the wall. She ignored me, left the room and the light went out. I was left in my waterproof coat, imprisoned on the bed, aching to relieve my bladder. I knew that again I wouldn't last the night. And tomorrow, I would have sixty strokes of the cane to face. If there ever was an all time low in my life, this was it.

## CHAPTER SEVEN

I spent that night in utter turmoil, I doubted my ability to survive the spanking that I was due to receive the next day. During the night my bladder opened and I released a stream of urine into my PVC panties. I slept only fitfully in the wet discomfort and growing terror of what was to come the following day. In the morning, Nurse Bowles and Amada Drew came into the dormitory to release the girls, but they left me harnessed.

"A warning for all of you girls, if any of you try to release Abbey or even speak to her, you'll take her place and receive her sixty strokes of the cane. You're being watched, I strongly suggest you keep away from her."

That was enough, even Zoe didn't dare to speak to me or try to help and I was left harnessed into my wet discomfort. The girls got washed and dressed and gradually the dormitory emptied. I was left laying harnessed to my bed wondering what was in store for me. Amaada Drew came back in carrying a pile of small white towels and left them next to my bed. Good God no, they were nappies, adult nappies.

After about an hour, when all of the girls would have been in class, Nurse Bowles came back into the dormitory with Miss Drew and the headmaster, Mr Murdoch. Without saying a word, and while he watched, they lifted my hips and pulled off my wet plastic panties, pulling faces and making comments about the smell. I closed my eyes with humiliation as they fastened one of the nappies around my hips, then they pulled a clean pair of plastic panties over the nappy. When they were done I opened my eyes to see Murdoch standing over me, grinning.

"In view of the fact that you cannot control yourself, Abbey, I have instructed that you be kept out of trouble. If you can learn to behave you'll be allowed out of bed and if there are no further incidents you'll gradually be released from the garments that must be irksome to you, the nappies and then the yellow mac. Until such time as you can manage that you stay as you are."

To my horror they left the room and left me harnessed and wearing an adult nappy. I lay there in my misery for hour after hour, until eventually the girls came in to get ready for bed. They still wouldn't speak to me out of terror of getting further punishment and I had to remain lonely and uncomfortable. I'd already wet the nappy and was doing my best not to shit in it to make matters worse. Then the nurse came in with her assistant. With a great show of disgust they changed my nappy again and pulled my pants back on, then left me for the night. Once more I spent a miserable, uncomfortable night. In the morning they came to change my nappy again and later in the morning the headmaster came to see me.

"Well, Abbey, what's it to be?"

"I'm sorry, Mr Murdoch, I'll behave, I promise. Please will you release me from this harness?"

He pretended to think for a moment, I could see he was loving the absolute control, the sexual thrill that his power over a mere defenceless girl gave him.

"When you are released you will be kept in nappies until you can behave like an adult, you realize that?"

I shuddered inside. "Yes, sir, I do."

"And of course you'll have to take your caning, sixty strokes on The Academy stage?"

My stomach churned, how the hell could I stand it? But I had to if I had any chance of escaping this torture.

"Yes, sir, I understand."

"Very well, I'll release you. Go straight to Nurse Bowles to get your nappy changed, then report to the stage and wait for me. Make sure you behave this time, Abbey."

"Yes, sir."

He went away and I got up from my cramped position and went to find Nurse Bowles in the infirmary. She smiled when she saw me looking so embarrassed.

"Lay on the examination table, Abbey and I'll change your nappy. Are you going for punishment afterwards?"

"Yes, Nurse Bowles," I replied courteously.

"Very good."

I lay down and she pulled down my waterproof panties and took off my nappy and changed it for a clean one. Then she pulled my panties back up and the skirts of my yellow mac down.

"You're ready now, go to the stage for punishment. I'll see you later when you need changing."

"Thank you, Nurse Bowles."

There was only one thing on my mind, not revenge, not escape, only to end the constant punishments so that I could get some of my life back. Nothing seemed as important at that moment as being a well behaved girl and ending the constant misery that my life had become. I was going to behave. When I got into the Academy hall all of the girls were assembled to watch what happened when girls misbehaved badly. Mr Murdoch was waiting on the stage next to the vaulting horse. I walked up the steps and stood before him.

"Are you ready, Abbey?"

"Yes, Mr Murdoch."

"Good."

He pushed me onto the vaulting horse and strapped my hands and ankles so that I couldn't move. I was positioned facing away from the audience so that they could all see what was happening to my rear. He pushed the skirts of my yellow mac over my head and I heard him addressing the girls.

"This is what happens when you repeatedly misbehave."

I felt him pulling down my plastic panties.

"This girl spends so much time harnessed to her bed that she has been put in nappies."

Of course, that was why he wanted me facing away from them, so that they could see my further humiliation. There was a collective sigh from the girls and I felt my face burning with the embarrassment of them knowing.

"Today she is to receive sixty strokes of the cane. If she behaves, she may be allowed to spend more time out of bed. She may even be allowed out of her nappies. She may be allowed out of her yellow mac, we'll see how she behaves."

He paused for effect. "If on the other hand she does not behave, she'll be kept restrained and the next punishment will be one hundred and twenty strokes of the cane."

I heard the collective gasp of horror from the girls. It was cruelty beyond belief, yet not one of us doubted that this monster, this sadist meant everything he said. My God, sixty strokes of the cane, and one hundred and twenty if I put a foot wrong again. But I wouldn't put a foot wrong, I was going to behave.

I felt him fumbling around my face and the gag was strapped over me.

"We don't want you crying out and upsetting the other girls, do we, Abbey?"

I shook my head and gurgled, it was all I could manage. Then I waited, my bare ass sticking up in the air in front of the whole Academy. I heard him walk away from me, ready to put force into the blow as he ran forward. Then he paused for a moment and I held my breath. His feet pounded as he began to run, oh please, give me the strength to endure this, then the incredible agony as the cane whacked down on my bare ass sending a shockwave all the way through my body. I struggled to get free, I couldn't stand another fifty nine of these, couldn't, but I was strapped and gagged to the horse. His feet moved back, slowly, then he ran forward and my ass erupted, on fire with the colossal, unbearable pain. The skirts of my yellow mac were over my face and I saw daylight as they were lifted back slightly to allow me to see, hope rose within me, but it was only Amanda Drew, she'd set the video camera on a tripod and had it running to video the expressions of agony on my gagged face. I looked at her beseechingly, please, help me, but then the massive pain shot through me as the next blow hammered on my rear. I was weeping now as blow after blow smashed into my rear. It felt sticky and I knew I would be bleeding, but no-one bothered to do anything to staunch the flow of blood.

"Are you going to behave now, Abbey?" Amy suddenly said.

I nodded my head vigorously.

"I'm to take over for the second half of your punishment, would you like me to make it easier for you?" she whispered. "Would you do anything, anything at all?"

I nodded again. I would too, anything she wanted to stop the agony.

"Very well, it's a promise."

The first half of my punishment ended, my ass was a torment of fiery agony. Amy took over the cane and began again, but she was as good as her word. The second thirty strokes were much more bearable, she managed it in such a way that no-one suspected she was pulling the blows. I was grateful to her and when she'd finished and she unfastened my straps and gag I wondered what she would want in return. She was a sadist, of that there was no doubt. What was the price for denying her a few minutes of sadism? She pulled my nappy over my ass, pulled up my plastic pants and looked at me.

"Come with me to the infirmary, Abbey, you've got some cuts that need treating," she said.

"Yes, Miss Drew. Thank you for punishing me."

She smiled as I followed her out. In the infirmary she told me to strip everything off.

"I mean everything, Abbey, every stitch, I need to give you a complete physical."

So that was it, she wanted my body. Well, she could have it, I'd do anything to avoid more punishment. I stripped off my clothes and stood before her, naked. She stroked each of my tits in turn.

"Lay on the treatment couch, Abbey, on your stomach."

I did as she told me and she started to gently rub cream into my wounds. It stung badly but I knew it needed to be done. She finished and I looked up, she was removing all of her clothes.

"Get down from the couch, I want you do to something for me."

I got down and she lay on her back on the rug.

"Go down on me, my darling, a caning always makes me feel horny and I'm bored with doing it myself. Don't use any hands, I want you to use your tongue to bring me to an orgasm."

I knelt over and put my head down between her legs, she pulled up her knees and parted her legs wide. Her cunt loomed in front of me and I was ready serve her, to do anything to behave. I licked inside her and found her clit, feeling her body arch as I ran my tongue slowly over it, she was already soaking wet. Then I sucked hard on her, tonguing, licking, sucking, working hard to satisfy her. I began to feel tired after a few minutes, I was still in shock from the beating, but she put a hand on my wounded ass and I lurched with shock and pushed my head further into her vagina, sucking harder, pushing my tongue along faster, working at her clit and being rewarded with the little moans that came from her to show that my efforts were working.

I was getting aroused myself but didn't know how I could do anything about it, I had to concentrate all of my energies on pleasing the woman between whose legs my mouth and tongue were doing their work. I must have slackened a little because her hand slapped down on my tortured ass again and I jumped with shock, then pushed harder again into her. I must have given her oral for more than half an hour, I was so numb and stiff with the constant effort, fearful of the sharp blow to my rear when I eased off a little, but finally after a huge effort she did reach an orgasm, no easy task when all I had to use was my mouth. Her hands wrapped around my head and pushed it hard into her crotch so that I couldn't release myself and I waited with my mouth and tongue embedded in her soaking vagina while she enjoyed me just being there. At last she released me.

Her eyes were a little wild and she looked at me with something of a predatory gaze.

"Are you aroused, Abbey? Tell me the truth."

I nodded. "Yes, yes, I am, Miss Drew."

She nodded. "Yes, I thought the taste of female cunt would do that to you. Stand up."

I stood. "Masturbate, Abbey. I want to see you do it."

I gaped at her. "Now, Miss?"

"Now. Do it."

"Yes, Miss." I reached down with my hand and touched my labia, feeling their warm softness, then went further, inside, my fingers brushed me clit and I shivered with the joy of touching myself in such a sensitive, sensual place. I should have been embarrassed, but somehow I wasn't. All I felt was an escape, I left the grim, agonizing reality of this place behind me and with the smell and the taste of her on my lips I drifted away to some magical place, a place where there was no caning, no pain, no excruciating imprisonment of humiliating nappies, just me and my fingers, touching, rubbing, warm and pleasing, responding to me exactly as I wanted, obeying my commands and ignoring everyone and everything. My mind drifted into a dark place of selfish pleasure where no-one mattered except me, at last I could be who I wanted to be, where I wanted and with whom I wanted. Then I came, a shattering, mind-shocking orgasm that caused my body to writhe and shake with passion and pleasure, a contrast so massive compared to what I had been through over the past few days. Then I felt dizzy, the last thing I remembered before I passed out was Amanda Drew's face staring at me with a sardonic smile stretching out her lips into a cruel imitation of a human being.

# CHAPTER EIGHT

I needed to spend a few days recovering, I'd been so badly beaten, bound and humiliated that I felt like crawling into a dark hole and never coming out. I even contemplated suicide, but only briefly, it was never a real option. I was a fighter, not a coward, I didn't retreat. I was a giver, not a taker. It was time to do some giving and less taking. But first I needed to recover my strength. So I spent several days behaving, the perfect young lady, meek and obedient, hard working and ready to instantly jump to do the bidding of the staff. It had the double effect of both lowering their guard and helping me to recover physically. I hated and loathed the constant discomfort of my physical predicament, but I conditioned my mind to ignore the sharp pain that shot through me when I sat down, the hideous wet feeling of being forced to wear nappies, and to know that everyone else knew, walking around in the yellow, hooded waterproof coat so that on the outside I stood out like a lighthouse beacon and on the inside I alternately perspired and froze. Zoe was ready and waiting for me to give the signal to move. We decided to do it one night when we should be able to get to the locked studio unseen. She had rigged her harness so that she could put her hand down and unclip it after she was locked in. While the others were asleep she got up, still wearing the harness and came over to me. She freed me from my harness and I unstrapped hers so that we were both free. There was one thing more, I went to the bathroom and removed the hated reminders of my bondage. Off came the yellow mac, the plastic underpants and the soaking nappy. I hid everything under the laundry basket in the bathroom and feeling a little better, got dressed and joined Zoe, who was already dressed and ready to go.

We crept through the dormitory and out of the door. Then along the corridor, moving silently and along to the staircase. We walked up the several flights of stairs that led to the top floor and across to the room that housed the studio. It wasn't empty. There was the sound of the cane hitting bare flesh, the sharp 'smack' as it connected with someone's rear. A female voice, "Oh God, do it to me again, please, more, much more."

The door was open a crack and we peered in. It was Amanda Drew, she was fastened to a wooden contraption so that her feet were on the floor, her hands also connected with the floor but her body was bent over in a bow shape. She had a huge dildo pushed into her cunt, so thick and long that it reached the floor, when she sagged and let the pressure off of her arms and legs, it obviously pushed into her even more. Julian Murdoch had hold of the cane and was standing over her, she must have received a good thrashing already, her ass was striped and bloody. But even more astonishing, Nurse Bowles was there, strapped over a vaulting horse, her wrists and ankles tied and her skirt pulled up and her panties down. She had a nasty looking gag in her mouth that prevented any kind of speech, by its shape it was some kind of an artificial penis jammed into her throat and held by the straps around her head. Murdoch had removed his pants and underwear, he was naked from the waist down. He turned and gave Nurse Bowles a hard blow with the cane that caused her to squirm in agony, then went to stand in front of Amanda.

"Now, dear, how would you like it, soft or hard?"

"Oh, hard, please, do it to me hard."

He smacked down with the cane, then again and again, as we watched he seemed to become possessed, lost all control, he was attacking her with a frenzy, her ass was running with blood now and she suddenly screamed loudly. "No, no more, that's enough, I can't take any more."

"Shut up, I'll decide when you've had enough."

'Whack', he brought the cane whistling down, and again, repeated blows and Amanda's voice was now one long, continuous scream of agony.

"If you can't shut up I'll shut you up," he snarled at her. Then he went to a box and got out a long, black rubber dildo gag, obviously the same as he had used for the nurse. Her eyes widened as she saw what he intended.

"No, not that, really, I can't do that, don't, please, aaahhhhhn…"

Then her voice was cut off as he thrust the long rubber dildo into her mouth and almost down her throat. He fastened the straps around her head and then looked satisfied at both of his mute victims.

"Now listen to me, you two useless cows. You came to me for work when you'd been thrown out of your last jobs, no-one would employ you. I took you on to work for me here, you both said you enjoyed a good spanking, now look at you, the first time you experience a bit of real pain you start snivelling like some of these useless girls. You should be ashamed of yourselves, I'll show you what a good spanking is."

He frightened us then as he laid about both women with his cane, slashing at them again and again so that their rears were covered in bloody stripes. It was obvious to assess the awful pain they were in, they heaved at the straps that held them, tears ran down their faces, but they were unable to utter a sound. I'd had enough.

"Zoe, I'm going to get help, he can't carry on attacking those helpless women."

"How will you do that?" she asked. "None of the teachers are likely to want to get involved, they're all terrified of Murdoch."

I wasn't thinking of the teachers, they were all spineless jellyfish for allowing what went on in this hellhole.

"I'm going to break into Murdoch's office while he's up here and try and find a phone, there must be one in there somewhere, I'm calling the police."

"Do you think that's wise, Murdoch will kill you if he finds out who did it?"

"I don't care, what's the alternative, let those women suffer?"

She nodded. "You're right. I'll stay here and keep an eye on things, if he goes away I'll try and free them."

I sprinted away along the corridor and down the stairs. I saw the headmaster's office ahead of me and ran towards it.

"What the hell are you doing out of bed?" a voice spat out.

I had run straight into Erica Rogers. The person who knew exactly what went on in that room upstairs, who aided the headmaster to make his pornographic videos. I knew it would be useless to try and ask her for help so I skidded to one side and tried to run around her. As I did I so I tripped on the polished floor and pitched headlong, landing headfirst against the wall. I was stunned, I must have been unconscious for a few minutes. When I came to Erica had put me into a restraint, a strap around my waist with a manacle either side for my wrists and a similar restraint on my ankles to hobble my legs.

"Erica, you can't get away with this," I said desperately. "You've gone over the top, what you're doing is illegal and you know it. This is kidnap and illegal imprisonment."

She laughed. "So what are you going to do about it, Abbey? Run for help?"

"I'll scream, I'll raise the whole school, someone will find out what you're doing."

"Yes, I thought you might do that."

She had a bundle of straps in her hand, held behind her back. When she brought it into view, I saw she had yet another of the terrible dildo gags like I'd seen Murdoch use on Nurse Bowles and Amanda Drew."

"Erica, Christ, no, don't, I could choke on that."

She shrugged and smiled, "So?"

Before I could get out a scream she pushed the vile, long rubber appendage into my mouth and all the way back to that it was pressing into my throat. It was all I could do to stop myself from choking. She tightened the straps around the back of my head and I felt the hard rubber pressing more firmly into my throat. I had to take short, tiny breaths to stop myself from choking, it was the only way I could breathe.

"Right, now that you're nicely packaged I'll take you to find Mr Murdoch. Why aren't you wearing your yellow coat, you're in punishment, you know you're supposed to wear it at all times?"

She smiled as I gurgled. "No, of course, you can't reply can you. Well, I'll get you kitted out before we go up. There are some coats hanging in Nurse Bowles' sick room, we'll find you one there."

She took hold of the belt and pulled me along towards the infirmary. I could only shuffle in tiny, mincing steps, taking shallow breaths, it was a terrifying experience. Erica opened the door and pulled me inside, then found a yellow rubber coat.

"I'll get this on you, as you're a bit tied up," she smiled, "You can wear it like a cape. Rather stylish, don't you think?"

She zipped the coat around me, pulled the hood over my head and tied it under my chin.

"You're ready, let's go and see the headmaster."

It was a pain wracked, shuffling journey up the stairs, gagged and hobbled, unable to use my hands to keep my balance. Erica dragged me along and kept me upright when I stumbled. When we got to the room where the women were being held and spanked there was no sign of Zoe. I hoped to God she hadn't been caught. Maybe she'd abandoned me, I couldn't really blame her, there was enough suffering in this place without her sticking her head up high enough to be caught. I was dragged into the room. The two women were still gagged and strapped to the devices, their asses bleeding badly. Murdoch was sitting at a desk writing, he looked up, surprised.

"What's all this, Erica?"

"I found Abbey wandering around downstairs, Headmaster. She had no business being out of bed, I don't know what she was doing. I believe she's in punishment, but she wasn't wearing her yellow coat so after I'd secured her I put one on her."

"Yes, I see. You've done well. Abbey, what have you to say for yourself, do you like being punished, is that why you keep breaking the regulations?"

I shook my head, I was unable to speak.

"I think you must enjoy this. You seem to keep challenging the system here, the only explanation is that you're not suffering enough from the punishments you've been given so far. Obviously we need to make it much harsher for you so that you'll start to obey.

I was shaking my head with fear, the guy was crazy, a stark, raving loony.

"Erica, release Amanda from that device and put Abbey in her place, would you? I assume you're no virgin, are you dear? No, of course you're not."

I tried to shuffle away, I was mortally terrified now but Murdoch took hold of me and held me while Erica undid Miss Drew's straps and eased her off of the frame, the huge, floor mounted dildo stood there stark and threatening. Amanda was in a bad way as she struggled to her feet.

"I'll take the gag off you, Amanda, but if you start whining you'll be back in the frame, do you understand?"

She nodded and he unstrapped the gag from her mouth. I saw her massaging her jaws where they'd been held in such a stiff position for so long.

"May I get dressed, Headmaster?" she asked him meekly.

It was as if the beating had totally removed her character, she was behaving like a meek, terrified slave, which I guess she was.

"I suppose you may, but shouldn't you thank me for such a delightful experience?"

She shuddered. "Thank you for such a wonderful spanking, Headmaster."

"You're welcome," he smiled. "Now get yourself cleaned up and dressed, and then you can go."

He turned his attention to me. "Now, Missy, you need a much stronger lesson in discipline, I think. Erica, put her onto the frame."

She took off my yellow mac and pulled my skirt up and tucked it into the straps around my waist. I struggled to fight her off but without the use of my limbs I was entirely helpless. I couldn't even cry out and every movement threatened to choke me. She pulled down my panties and then Murdoch helped to lower me onto the apparatus, he guided the huge dildo into my cunt. It was shocking, a fearful, terrifying experience being invaded by that monstrous object. They unstrapped my wrists and ankles and re-fastened them to the floor restraints and then let me go. Immediately, the monster dildo pressed into me and I had to hold myself up to stop it completely impaling me. I couldn't escape, couldn't cry out, I was more in their power than ever before, worse, I began to feel the terrible discomfort of the straps and dildos biting into me more than ever. I knew I wouldn't be able to stand it for long. Would I lose my mind in this terrible punishment chamber? Would I wind up like Amanda, an obedient automaton? Even then, I determined that no way would I allow this sick psycho to do that to me. Whatever he did, no matter how much pain and terror he inflicted, I was going to fight it.

His whip cracked down and a searing pain shot through me, he hit so hard that it drove my cunt down onto the dildo and it pressed harder inside me, so I had to press up with my hands and legs more to get the pressure off of me. Then again, and again. Ten strokes, delivered with all of his strength. I could feel the thin trickle of blood as it ran down my cheeks and down my legs.

"How was that for starters, Abbey? Did that make you think about behaving at all?"

I said nothing, couldn't say anything. Then 'whack', ten more strokes, the pain was horrifying in its intensity.

"I asked you a question, Abbey, are you having a change

of heart?"

Well fuck you, you perverted sick asshole, I thought. With the last will that I could summon, I shook my head firmly.

"Well that's a shame, I'll have to keep going. Nurse Bowles, what do you think, perhaps fifty hard strokes of the cane, would that do the trick, would that persuade this young lady to follow orders?"

Charlotte Bowles shook her head, clearly she was as terrified as I was, or almost.

"You think not? But fifty strokes is not so hard, let me show you."

She was shaking her head in mortal terror, but she may as well have not bothered. He stood over her and brought the cane down repeatedly. Tears ran freely down her face and every time the cane struck her she jerked with the fearful pain that was being inflicted. I counted each and every terrible stroke, by the time he reached fifty the nurse was slumped over the frame, almost unconscious. Murdoch lifted up her head to look at her face.

"My, my, I think you've gone to sleep, you need waking up."

He brought the cane down with all of his strength and struck her in the middle of her wounded rear. She jerked and I could see she had returned to consciousness.

"That's better. Now, fifty strokes isn't so bad, is it? Will it help make this young lady respond better to school discipline, or do you need more persuasion?"

She nodded her head enthusiastically.

"Yes, I thought you'd agree. You're obviously learning yourself. When I've finished Abbey's punishment I'll release you, you need to get ready for the next school day, we can't have a school without a nurse, can we?"

She shook her head.

"But in the meantime, I think you should see how the punishment you agreed with works on Abbey."

## CHAPTER NINE

I understood it all now. He was quite mad, totally insane, truly a certifiable lunatic. I was worried that if I didn't get out of this room before long he was capable of killing me. Then he came over to me with his cane.

"Now for your punishment, Abbey. It's for your own good, it will help you be an obedient young lady. Nurse Bowles thinks so too."

Then he brought the cane down and I suffered fifty of the most agonizing strokes imaginable. I had to press hard against the monstrous dildo pushed inside of me, but that meant that I had to take all of the weight of the blows without my body sagging at all to absorb the shock. When he had delivered the fiftieth blow he stopped. I felt the room starting to spin, I was in danger of blacking out but I knew I couldn't, I would complete my impalement and quite possibly die. I saw Murdoch release Nurse

Bowles and she stiffly walked out of the room, she was obviously in terrible pain, shaking with both the agony of the beating and the terror of the man that had inflicted it. Murdoch made a few notes in a book, and then went towards the door.

"I'm leaving you to think about your situation, Abbey. I'll come back in the morning. When you have decided to be totally obedient, to obey all of the school regulations without question, you may beg me to give you another fifty strokes for all of the trouble you have caused. Until then, you can stay like that and you'll be beaten anyway. It's up to you, but I'd seriously think about changing your attitude."

He left the room and I was on my own, strapped over the dildo that pressed into me. I had to keep conscious, had to support my body, otherwise I could suffer serious injury or death. It was a night of sheer terror and agony, I counted every second. In the morning Murdoch came back.

"Well, Abbey, did you have a comfortable night?" he sneered.

I stayed still, did he want me to nod or shake my head, what did he want me to do? All I knew was that I'd have to get out of this.

"Have you decided to beg for the fifty strokes to forgive your disobedience?"

I nodded. I'd already decided that I'd do anything at

all to get out of this. Afterwards I was going to nail the fucker, one way or the other, but first things first.

"You're very wise, I'm sure this will be good for you."

I had to endure fifty more terrifying, tortuous strokes of his cane, I knew that my ass would now look like raw mince. Towards the end I thought I was in danger of having to collapse against the dildo and let it completely impale me and it was only by using the last reserves of my strength that I managed to keep it from penetrating all the way inside me.

"I'm going to release you now, Abbey, remember, you are treading on very thin ice. The least disobedience and you'll be strapped back onto this device, it's not very comfortable, is it?"

He undid the straps and helped ease me off of the dildo. Gratefully, I stood upright and waited while he unstrapped the gag. I went to take a step but I couldn't move and I started to massage some circulation back into my arms and legs.

"Well, Abbey?"

"Thank you for the punishment, Mr Murdoch."

"Good girl. Put your mac on and go downstairs, you can go straight to your lesson. There's no need to sit down, the teachers will understand."

"Yes, Mr Murdoch."

"Excellent."

I put on the yellow mac and zipped it up, tied the hood

and staggered out of the room and down the stairs. I found my classroom and went in, the lesson had started and the teacher nodded to me to take my place. When I stood in front of my desk he understood, of course. By lunchtime I was trembling, the pain and constriction of the punishment, the lack of food and sleep had all contrived to leave me weak and barely able to keep going. There was no sign of Zoe, I wondered had they caught her, was she being held, strapped down in one of the rooms in this hellhole?

As I was about to sit down to eat, Nurse Bowles came to see me.

"Abbey, I need you to come with me."

The expression on her face was awful, she looked frightened out of her wits, she was shaking with fear. I got up and followed her to the infirmary. Murdoch was there.

"Ah, Abbey. You were told to wear nappies, weren't you?"

I nodded. "Yes, but…"

"No buts, put one on her, Nurse."

I stood mute while the nurse pulled down my plastic pants and fastened a nappy around my waist.

"Good. Abbey, what do we do here when you are disobedient?"

"You spank us, Mr Murdoch."

"I see. You were disobedient, should I spank you?"

I was trapped, I knew I was a hair's breadth from being strapped back onto the terrible device in the room upstairs.

"Yes, Mr Murdoch."

"Very well. Report to the hall at three o'clock. I believe you are due for one hundred and twenty strokes. Let's hope it's enough to complete your obedience training."

He stalked out of the room. I looked at the nurse. "I can't take it, he'll kill me."

"But what can I do?" she asked desperately. "You saw what he did to me, and to Amanda. There's no way off the island, we're all completely in his power."

She had changed completely as the full impact of the headmaster's psychotic behaviour became apparent to her and she realised that this was no longer a game. There was a knock at the door and a girl came into the room. It was Zoe.

"What happened to you, I thought you'd abandoned me?"

"No, I heard them bringing you back when they caught you in the night, I ran off, otherwise they'd have caught me too. Look, I couldn't find a phone but I managed to get a message out to my cousin Jason by email. I've tried to convince him how serious it is and asked him to call the police, but before he could email back I had to switch off the computer when I heard someone coming. I don't know if he understood that I was serious, he may thought I was joking."

I told her about the night I'd had, about the one hundred and twenty strokes I was facing.

"In that case, we're done for," she said.

"You mean I'm done for."

She pulled a face. "I'm sorry."

It wasn't really her fault, this was a place of unfathomable terror, where fear of unending punishment and torture stalked the whole building. I felt so weak and tired, my head must have started to slump forward.

"You won't need a sleeping tablet tonight, Abbey," Nurse Bowles said. "You look so very tired."

Brilliant.

"I've got an idea. You do keep sleeping tablets and stuff like that?"

"Yes, of course," the nurse replied. "Sometimes the girls are in such pain that I give them something to help them sleep."

"Can we get something into Murdoch's afternoon tea?"

Everyone knew about the afternoon tea ritual, when the nurse had to stop whatever she was doing and take him a pot of tea on a silver tray with a plate of biscuits. She blanched.

"He'd kill me if he found out."

"Look, he could kill us all anyway, don't you think he's gone completely psycho, totally over the top?"

She thought for a few moments. "I see what you mean. Yes, ok, I'll do it. What then?"

"When he's knocked out, get word to the staff, they must all be terrified of him too."

She nodded. "I'll do that."

"Tell them to leave it to us girls, we'll deal with him ourselves, I think we're owed that much."

She shook her head. "They may not go for it."

"In that case, when the police are involved, and they will be, I'll make sure they're all named as accessories to kidnap, imprisonment and abuse."

She paled. "You're right, I'll persuade them, don't worry."

I had a quiet word with Zoe and explained what I had in mind. "We must have those videos, we'll need the evidence to get him convicted as an abusing kidnapper as well as a pornographer."

She nodded. "I'll get some of the girls and tell them to go and get them."

"Good. We'll need about six of us to put this into effect."

When we went into his office, Murdoch was slumped over his desk, fast asleep. Good, that was stage one completed. Zoe was carrying a set of school uniform.

"Right, strip him and put him into uniform, he'll look good in a short tartan skirt and blouse, especially with plastic panties underneath."

When he was ready, they got the heavy black shoes onto his feet and zipped him into a yellow waterproof coat and fastened the hood. I rummaged in the drawers of his desk, certain I would find what I needed there. Sure enough, a black rubber penis gag with straps. I pushed it into his mouth and fastened it behind his head. Then six of us carried the still-sleeping form to the school hall and up onto the stage.

"Strap him to the frame," I said to them.

They giggled and fixed his ankles and wrists to the spanking frame. He was already starting to stir, his eyes wide, especially when he found that he couldn't use his hands or feet and couldn't even speak. His voice came out in a series of furious gurgles.

I stood in front of him and lifted his head.

"Remember me, Julian? The thing is, the girls and I think that you've been a naughty boy. The only cure for that is a few strokes with a riding crop, isn't that what you say? I'm going to get the whole school in here and we'll see how you enjoy your own medicine."

He started to panic, pulling and twisting to try and get away, gurgling louder to try and protest, but he was wasting his time, he should have known that. The spanking horse with its straps was his own invention. Two of the girls went to spread the word of a special assembly and soon the hall was filling up with girls. The teachers had been warned by Nurse Bowles, they knew that the game was up and they didn't dare to protest. They were all on a precipice, in danger of prosecution and long jail sentences.

I lifted up his head so that they could all see who was strapped to the frame, they gasped. It was unprecedented, at that moment any authority that Murdoch had in the school evaporated. He looked utterly ridiculous, a grown man dressed like a schoolgirl in the short tartan skirt, his plastic panties pulled down to his ankles, the yellow coat pulled up ready and his ass exposed for what was to come.

"How many should we give him, girls, this very naughty boy? Fifty?"

There were shouts in the hall, a hundred, five hundred, a thousand."

It was very tempting. "I think we'll start with a hundred."

I saw him flinch, his eyes widened with horrified anticipation that he was about to get a painful taste of his own medicine.

"I'll do the first ten," I shouted out. "I need volunteers to do ten each. I wouldn't want him to get an easy time because my arm gets tired."

Less than a minute later there was a long line waiting to come up to the stage. There must have been thirty girls.

"That's a shame," I said to Murdoch. "They'll want to do ten strokes each, that means you'll get about three hundred. But remember what you said, it's good for you, it teaches discipline?"

He was still writhing in the straps, his eyes filled with terror gurgling and drooling through the gag, spittle dripping onto the floor.

"I think we'll begin, enjoy it, Murdoch, you know how you love dishing it out."

I whacked him hard with all of my strength, the sound of the blow seemed to echo around the hall. His body jumped with the shock of the blow. Then again and again, ten very hard whacks and I could see the red stripes on his ass beginning to seep blood. Excellent, he was getting a real taste of his own discipline.

"Come on, next one up, lay it on as hard as you possibly can, you know how important he thinks it is."

The next girl took the riding crop and started. Once more the sound of the thrashing echoed around the hall. Murdoch was sobbing now, his body was shaking with terror and pain, tears pouring down his face. Good, the worse it was for him, the more he'd realize how terrible the pain and torture he'd inflicted on us had been. The afternoon wore on and still the thrashing with the riding crop continued, at one stage he seemed to pass out and the Nurse was called to give him some smelling salts to wake him up.

"We wouldn't want you to miss any of your punishment, would we? We all know the importance you attach to it."

He shook his head miserably. Finally, the last girl had delivered her ten whacks and Murdoch was left strapped over the frame. Zoe came up to me.

"What are we going to do now, Abbey? If we let him

go he could make a lot of trouble."

"Don't worry, I've worked that out. Did you get the videos?"

"Yes, the girls got them, they're guarding them. Amanda and Erica tried to stop them, but they locked them in a closet, they'll keep them there for now. Are the police really coming?"

"Yes, Nurse Bowles slipped away and put a call through on Murdoch's personal phone, he keeps it locked away in his desk drawer."

We released Murdoch's ankles and fastened them back into the travelling restraints. While two girls held each of his arms, I unstrapped them and fitted his wrists into the waist restraints. Then I released him from the frame.

"How did you enjoy that, Murdoch?"

Of course, he was still gagged, I reached behind his head and unstrapped him.

"I'll kill you, I'll murder the lot of you for this," he shouted. He was burbling now, raving, totally gone.

"I don't think so, my friend, you'll be locked up in a prison cell."

Then I had an idea. "Let's release him and take him for a walk around the grounds, he's got his yellow mac on, let's parade him for everyone to see.

I loosened his leg restraints so that he was able to take short steps. Then we led him outside and started to walk him around the school grounds. In the distance I could see a police launch approaching.

"Let them see you in your full glory, Mr Murdoch. Girls, let's get him out of the mac and then put his straps back on so that he can't escape. He can go to jail wearing school uniform, it's obviously so important to him."

We held him and removed his mac, then strapped his wrists back to the belt. In the school uniform of short tartan skirt, blouse, socks and heavy shoes, he was indeed a picture. We took him down to the jetty and handed him over to the police. He protested and shouted, but Nurse Bowles was with us and explained everything he had been doing at the school.

## CHAPTER TEN

The cops looked at him in total disgust. "So he's enjoying spanking defenceless girls and even wears girls school uniform himself. They'll have a lot of fun with you when they get you to the nick, my friend."

They put him in the boat and two strong coppers held him firmly. He looked positively comical sat there in his tartan skirt and school blouse, he was handcuffed so couldn't do anything about it. When he moved position, I could see the plastic pants showing underneath the hem of his skirt. Lovely. His face was a reward for at least some of the misery and pain he'd caused us, he clearly knew what he was facing when he was put in jail, sex offenders didn't usually enjoy their stay in prison. The sergeant in charge came back onto the jetty.

"You'll all need to make statements, I'll have to send a team over here. What's all this about videos?"

We told him about the room full of pornographic DVDs, recordings of the girls being spanked and in other compromising positions. His face hardened. "Yes, we'll be having long conversations with the headmaster. Don't you have any way of getting on and off the island, no boat?"

I looked around, sure enough, the boat had gone. Of course, Amanda and Erica. I told him about the two women, both accomplices of Murdoch in his perverted enterprises.

"Don't worry, they won't get far, we'll trace the boat and put out a call for them from the mainland. This launch is too small for passengers, we'll bring you back in the larger boat we send over, will that be soon enough for you?"

I nodded. "That'll be fine, some of the better teachers are still there, and Nurse Bowles who wasn't really a part of the porn racket. We'll be ok."

Their boat slowly backed away from the jetty, then turned and headed at speed for the mainland. I went back to the school with the other girls and we started the hunt for our personal possessions, most importantly our clothes. We found them locked away in a storeroom and I was able to put on my own stuff and begin to feel more human. We wanted to build a bonfire of the school clothes but I remembered at the last moment that they may be needed for evidence. That was a serious reminder that there would be a trial and evidence would be needed to clinch the conviction of Murdoch and keep him off the streets for a good time to come. We broke open filing cabinets and found every document we could lay hands on, there were sickening photos, more videos, even several journals listing each day's punishments with names and numbers of strokes. It was in Murdoch's handwriting and on its own was probably enough to convict him. We helped ourselves to some of his personal food stocks and had something of a party, even discovering Murdoch's booze cabinet. Times had certainly changed as we danced and sang around the school building. In the morning the police returned in a larger boat, a ferry, and they took us back to the mainland where we made statements. When I came out of the police station my parents were there waiting.

"Abbey, darling," my mom rushed forward. "I'm so sorry, we've only just been told."

"Really. So you know that Murdoch will be put on trial for kidnap and child abuse?"

"Yes, we heard."

"So you know that anybody that helped him to kidnap the girls and spirit us away to this island might stand trial with him?"

Dad looked startled. "But surely you don't blame us?"

"No? Was it someone else that fixed up for me to be drugged and kidnapped?"

He didn't reply.

They took me home and by mutual consent nothing more was said. I was treated like a royal princess, nothing was too much for them to do for me. They knew damn well that I could bring the roof down on their heads if I chose to. One thing didn't change. I wasn't obedient. Whichever particular idiot or pervert honestly thought that spanking a girl to that extent, if at all, was going to change anything, I wondered? The only thing it did change for me was that I became harder, tougher and less inclined than before to obey them, not that they tried it on too much. A week after we got back, David Green, the boy I'd been caught with in boarding school on that fateful visit that started all of the trouble, made contact by email. Did I want to make a date, he asked me? I emailed back and asked him to phone. When he called, Mom and Dad were sat in the same room as me and could hear the call.

"David, you want to come over, yeah, that would be great. Hang on, I'll ask my parents."

I looked at them. "David wants to come over and I'd like a bit of privacy, would you two fix up to go out tomorrow evening?

"What are you talking about," Dad blustered. "This is our house."

"Dad, I can get you out of here permanently if I want, do you want me to call the police and make a complaint of accessory to drugged kidnap?"

It took him all of thirty seconds to truly understand the way things were. This obedience thing could be a lot of fun, you just needed to go about it the right way. The following evening Mom and Dad went out, they didn't look terrifically happy about it but that was too bad, they owed me, big time.

We sat together, David and me, and I told him about The Academy.

"You can't be serious, they were that cruel?"

"Oh yes, a bunch of crazy perverts, especially the headmaster."

"So what kind of sicko wants to see girls being spanked, or even be spanked themselves?"

I smiled. "You'd be surprised, it's not all bad, it can be quite, well, exciting, I suppose. In small doses."

"Really, that's amazing."

"Yeah, I'll show you my stripes, if you like."

His eyes goggled as I pulled down my panties and let him examine where I'd been so badly spanked with the cane."

"Jesus," he said as he touched the stripes. "This is awful. I don't get it, how anyone could enjoy it"

Did he honestly think I didn't know what he was thinking? His voice had gone hoarse and I swear I could see a hard lump in his pants. Oh yeah?

"David, would you like to try it?"

"Try it, try what, not spanking you, no, I couldn't do

that."

"I meant I'll give you a spanking, you can see how it feels, I can tell you're really excited by it."

"No, I'm not."

"So why has your penis grown rock hard since we've been talking about it?"

He blushed bright red. "Well, yeah, it is a bit, you know, that would be really cool, to experience something like that, right..."

"I know. I'll get you ready for it and give you a spanking."

He was still a bit hesitant, but then agreed to do it. Except when I told him that it meant he'd need to do the whole thing, wear my school clothes, I had a uniform from the previous school, short skirt, blouse, the whole deal. And he'd need to be strapped down. In the end I persuaded him and I helped him undress and put on my panties, short skirt, bra and blouse, long socks and shoes.

"Abbey, I feel ridiculous."

"Don't worry, no one can see you. Bend over the back of the armchair."

I'd found some straps and I fastened his ankles and wrists, he was totally powerless. Then I had an idea, I went and found my dildo and some thick tape, cut a hole in it and pulled the dildo partially through. Then I put it in his mouth. He hadn't seen it coming and his eyes bulged, he gurgled and dribbled but was totally gagged.

"You see, David, that's the way they did it to me and

you said you wanted the whole experience, so there you go. Wait there and I'll find a cane."

As if he had any choice except to wait. I went and found a whippy cane that Mom used for supporting her houseplants. I tried swishing it a couple of times in front of David, I smiled as he winced each time it came near him.

"What's the matter, doesn't my little girl want to have her ass caned?" I grinned at him.

He went red with frustration and rage, good, he'd wanted it and he was going to get it.

"They gave me sixty hard strokes once, but that might be a bit much for you to start off with. How about twenty good ones, that should be enough. Will you be an obedient little girl after twenty strokes?"

He glared at me and I went behind him and slashed down, once, twice, five times in all, I used all of my strength and the slap of the cane as it whipped across his ass sounded loud in the room. He was writhing with the agony of it, maybe he didn't think it was such a good idea? I went and stood in front of him.

"Now, I'll ask you again, will twenty strokes be enough to make you an obedient little girl?"

He nodded his head frantically, up and down.

"Good, I think so too. Let's try it and see how we go."

I went back behind him and brought the cane down, again and again, after another ten strokes I checked his face, he was weeping with pain and humiliation, his eyes tight shut. And there was something else in his face, Christ, it was lust. Well, well. So my boyfriend had found a new way to get his juices flowing.

"You're doing fine, I'm going to give my little girl the rest of her punishment, or do you think I should round it up to thirty?"

He opened his eyes, his expression was a mixture of pain and hope.

"Very well."

I went back around and started again, slashing down as hard as I could. Again and again I brought the cane down on the white flesh of his ass, now turning red with the familiar red stripes. There was even a thin trickle of blood, dear, dear, I must be getting good at this. Finally I was done, I put the cane back to where I had found it and went to release David. He looked so cool with his dildo strapped into his mouth, his short skirt rucked up over his waist, his striped ass showing above his legs with their white socks and school shoes, I had an idea.

"David, I want to try something, if I release your hands you won't try to fight me, will you?"

He shook his head.

"Ok, but let me warn you, if you try anything I'll give you another thirty and keep you there until my parents come home."

I saw him shudder, the threat was enough. I released

his wrists and pushed his body so that he was standing behind the chair, his ankles still strapped to the legs, his mouth still gagged with the dildo. Then I re-fastened his wrists, but this time I used the belts to fasten them behind his back.

"Stand there, don't move, I won't be a second."

I took down my panties and rucked up my own skirt, then I pushed myself between him and the chair. I guided his hard cock into my cunt and just let it stay there for a few moments. He was totally helpless, gagged, beaten, bleeding, bound, he couldn't do anything, I was totally in control.

Then I started to fuck him, sliding backwards and forwards slowly on his shaft. He moaned through the gag and I carried on, I heard him start to pant.

"David, don't come, I don't want you ending this yet."

His eyes were wild with lust, I knew he couldn't last much longer. There was only one thing for it. I slapped his bare, wounded ass. Right on the wounds, he reacted as if I'd given touched him with a blowtorch. But his lust subsided, at least for now. He couldn't object, that was the marvellous thing. He was mine, to punish or fuck as I pleased. I started sliding along his shaft again, I knew that I was dangerously close to climaxing, but at least we girls can do it again and again. I was wet, soaking wet with my vaginal juices almost pouring out of me. Then I did come, groaning and squirming, the wonderful elated feeling surging over me and enveloping my body. Then I sensed once again that he was about to come and I gave him five stinging slaps. Down boy, I'm not finished with you yet! I checked the clock and kept fucking him, after an hour and a half he was a total and utter wreck, I decided to let him have his release.

"Ok, David, you can come now, I think I've had enough."

I saw the gratitude in his eyes as I slid along him faster and faster, his cock grew even harder, rock hard and then almost instantly he climaxed inside me and I felt his hot semen filling me, it was as if he'd never stop. Finally he sagged against me. I unstrapped him and gently pulled my school clothes off him. Then I helped him back into his own clothes. He seemed to be stunned, lost, out of this world. Wow!

"David, did you enjoy that, the spanking and everything, the sex? Would you like to try it again sometime?"

He looked down to the floor, he couldn't face me, but I heard his hoarse reply.

"Please, yes."

THE END

CPSIA information can be obtained at www.ICGtesting.com
Printed in the USA
LVOW06s0835210713

343878LV00001B/141/P